UNTIL I'M SAFE IN YOUR ARMS

The Welwyn Marriage Wager
Book 1

By
Jenna Jaxon

Text by Jenna Jaxon
Cover by Kim Killion Designs

Dragonblade Publishing, Inc. is an imprint of Kathryn Le Veque Novels, Inc.
P.O. Box 23
Moreno Valley, CA 92556
ceo@dragonbladepublishing.com

Produced in the United States of America

First Edition May 2023
Trade Paperback Edition

ARE YOU SIGNED UP FOR DRAGONBLADE'S BLOG?

You'll get the latest news and information on exclusive giveaways, exclusive excerpts, coming releases, sales, free books, cover reveals and more.

Check out our complete list of authors, too!

No spam, no junk. That's a promise!

Sign Up Here

www.dragonbladepublishing.com

Dearest Reader;

Thank you for your support of a small press. At Dragonblade Publishing, we strive to bring you the highest quality Historical Romance from some of the best authors in the business. Without your support, there is no 'us', so we sincerely hope you adore these stories and find some new favorite authors along the way.

Happy Reading!

CEO, Dragonblade Publishing

Additional Dragonblade books by Author Jenna Jaxon

The Welwyn Marriage Wager Series
Until I'm Safe in Your Arms (Book 1)

The Lyon's Den Series
Pride of Lyons

Dedication

To Robert Alexander and Emma Washer Jackson, my great-grandparents, and Charles Saunders and Bessie Mae Jackson, my grandparents.

Thank you for giving the Jackson family its start.

I hope I make you proud.

PROLOGUE

London
August, 1860

"AND THIS GAME is called what, Tom?" Captain Alexander Bancroft, of Her Majesty's 30th Cambridgeshire Regiment of Foot, tapped his cards on the table, then commenced shuffling them absently. The drawing room in his grandfather, the Duke of Welwyn's, house in Mayfair was crowded this afternoon with Alex and five of his cousins. As the duke had yet to put in an appearance, the six of them had agreed to fill the time learning a new form of poker from their youngest cousin, Thomas Weston.

"Draw poker. How many cards do you want, Yule?" Tom held his hand suspended over the deck, his gaze on his older cousin. "It's been around Virginia for a while, but I just learned it on my last trip across the pond. Yule?"

A perturbed look on his face, Ulysses Quartermain studied his cards, then sighed. "Two, no three."

Tom laid one card on the table in front of his cousin, then another.

"Wait, just two." Yule frowned at his hand.

"Well, is it two or three?"

"Just two." Shaking his head, Yule discarded then stuck the

two new cards into his hand. He glanced at the clock, its hands standing at a quarter to two. "When's Grandfather putting in an appearance? I was supposed to call round at my club at two."

"Whenever he damn well pleases. And we'd better all be here when he does." Alex, the oldest of the group, grasped his tokens and let the metal counters run through his fingers. Their grandfather was quite the tyrant, in a good-natured way. But it didn't do to cross him at all. "Does anyone know what bee he's got in his bonnet this time?"

All his cousins shook their heads simultaneously.

"He's been pleased as a weasel ever since Henry got married." Yule was rearranging his cards and frowning. "So there's no reason I know of to call us all here. Do I bet yet?"

"Not yet. Francis, how many cards?" Tom doggedly kept the deal going. "I hope it doesn't have to do with that Lord Stonebridge business. None of us would ever contemplate putting our houses up as collateral in a wager. Well, those of us who actually own houses." He glanced first at Saunders, Lord Mckay, Sandy to all of them, who'd inherited a castle in Scotland, then at Julius, Lord Boxted, who'd inherited a number of estates when his father died.

Julius threw his hands up. "Not I, said the cat. I love a wager as well as the next man, but I'm not fool enough to put up property on a bet."

"My mother would put a Scottish curse on me if I ever did such a thing," Sandy said. "The only time I get to gamble at all is when I'm here with all of you. She won't allow a single deck of cards in the castle, save when we entertain, which is seldom, I have to say." He studied his cards. "I'll take three, Tom."

"Don't you live in London now, Sandy?" Alex contemplated his cousin with a keen eye.

"I do. Thank you, Tom." Sandy tossed his discard onto the growing pile then carefully fitted the new cards into his hand. "I have to, Alex. How else am I to be a fashionable English gentleman if I can't smoke, drink, or gamble? My mother abhors all three. Hence, here I am."

"So am I, young whippersnapper." The Duke of Welwyn strode magnificently into the drawing room, a tall, imposing figure in an excellently cut gray suit, who looked quite dapper despite his advanced age. The gruff manner of the words notwithstanding, there was still underlying affection in their grandfather's tone.

All six cousins rose as one.

"Good afternoon, Grandfather."

"Good to see you, Grandfather."

"How d'ya do, Grandfather?"

Each of them murmured a polite greeting, holding their eagerness in check. A difficult feat, Alex knew, as they were all rife with curiosity as to why they'd been summoned.

"Take your seats, except Alex."

Alex stopped, mid-sitting, and straightened up. "Yes, Grandfather?"

"Pour everyone a round, would you?" Grandfather leaned against the tall-backed, tufted black leather chair, bespoke especially for him.

Well, he could use one about now, and the rest of them looked the same. Alex quickly set out seven cut-crystal tumblers with a W engraved on them and began pouring good-sized tots of a fine vintage cognac. Might as well hit this head-on. "Why did you wish to see us all, Grandfather?"

"Because I'm dying, Alexander." Grandfather took his glass and downed the contents with a practiced hand.

All the cousins stared at him in shock, then sent furtive glances at the others around the room. Then, almost as if they'd rehearsed it, everyone rose, grabbed their glasses, and knocked back the cognac.

The smooth brandy produced a steady burn all the way down to Alex's stomach, providing some much needed comfort. If he'd known what his grandfather was going to announce, he'd have doubled the amount of liquor he'd poured. "What do you mean?"

A smile hitched up one side of Grandfather's mouth. "Just that, my boy. I'm dying. Mr. Thomas Peacock, a most eminent physician in the study of the heart, tells me that mine will give out within the year."

"But Grandfather..."

"Are you certain this man isn't a quack?"

"He can't be sure of this, can he?"

The din of his cousins' voices was enough to make Alex grab the decanter once more and pour a more generous slug into the tumbler.

"You look fine, Grandfather. The blasted man's daft."

"Good God." Tom plucked the decanter out of Alex's hands and poured himself another shot. "Isn't there anything that can be done?"

"I'm getting ready to do the only thing I can do to give myself peace of mind when my time comes." Grandfather shot a look at Tom. "Hand me that decanter, please." Tom gave it over and Grandfather poured himself a hefty—well, almost half—glass of the brandy. "I'm going to set you," he swept his hand dramatically around the circle that had formed about him, "all my grandsons of eligible age—a wager."

Despite their shock, all of them, Alex included, leaned in toward their grandparent. The word "wager" was like a flame to a moth as far as they were concerned.

"What's the wager?" Yule, the most pragmatic of them, would be the one to ask that.

Grandfather chuckled. "As I've got one foot in the grave, about to stare my Maker in the face, I wish to have my affairs in order before I 'shuffle off this mortal coil.'"

Cocking his head, Alex scrutinized their grandfather's face. He was simply too jovial for a man about to die. "I'd think you'd wish to consult your attorney about your affairs, not your grandsons."

"Oh, I've done that to be sure, my boy. Andrews is taking care of everything regarding the funeral and all the matters concerning the dukedom as it passes to Harry." Grandfather glanced around the room, seeming to wait for something.

"Why isn't Harry here?" Julius spoke up, a frown on his face. "Or his brother, John. Or our brother, Aubrey?"

"As I said, for this wager, they have to be eligible." Deep blue eyes flitting from one face to another, Grandfather sipped his drink and waited.

"Eligible for what?" Francis's frown matched his twin's.

"Marriage."

The word fell on Alex's ears like the crash of thunder during a storm. It electrified them all.

"Marriage?" Tom's voice reached an unusual height as the horror sunk in. "You want us *all* to get married?"

To Alex's astonishment, his grandfather nodded.

"But I'm scarcely in my twenties." Tom's panicked gaze roved from one face to the next, seeking support. "I've still got a lot of wild oats to sow. I don't want to get married yet."

"I'm sorry to hear that, Tom." Grandfather didn't look particularly sorry, and Tom was looking rather green at the moment. "Because for this wager to be valid, all six of you must participate. There can be no exceptions."

"What's this wager, Grandfather?" Alex held up a hand as Tom leaped forward to protest. He gave Yule and Sandy a stern look as well. The two most avid gamblers in a family known for its propensity to wager on anything under the sun might agree to marry the next woman they met on the street if the stakes of the wager were right. "We need to know before any of us will agree to it."

"Certainly, Alexander." The glint in his grandfather's eyes gave Alex no confidence at all. "A gentleman always makes himself familiar with the terms of the wager before agreeing to it." He nodded to his grandsons, and they all took seats, although none of them looked comfortable. Only Yule and Sandy appeared in any way excited.

"What brought this on, Grandfather?" Alex couldn't help

himself. All these events had come from out of the blue, and he didn't like it one bit.

"When we all attended Harry's wedding two months ago, I couldn't help but feel inordinately proud that the Quartermain name and the Welwyn title would go on as soon as Harry gets an heir." Grandfather chuckled. "I suspect *that* announcement will be made in the near future."

Alex had to agree. Harry was head over heels for his bride, Celeste. They hadn't returned from their honeymoon in Paris yet. Newlyweds in the city of love would likely mean only one thing: an heir.

"But I began to be concerned that none of my other grandsons of marriageable age had found the wedded bliss of your eldest cousin. And while my line is assured, your surnames have not been. For you all to be true Quartermains, with unimpeachable honor, your own surnames must be carried on throughout time. Therefore, I have devised a plan to marry you all off within the year."

"Within the year?" Francis's horror might have been comical had it not been shared by all of them in the room.

"That is the wager." Grandfather's smile could not have been more evil. The man had managed to hit upon the one way to ensure that all six of his grandsons would agree to those terms. None of them had ever been able to resist a wager. "Each of you must marry within a year from today's date, August 22, 1860, in order to collectively win the prize."

"And this prize is...?" Tom had found his voice at last, shaky though it was.

Grandfather gazed around the room slowly, allowing it to rest briefly on each grandson. "A payment of ten thousand pounds each, along with free title to an estate of your choosing—either one of my holdings outside the entail, or any reasonable estate available for purchase—a new carriage, and a new cabriolet." He paused to stare at Tom until his attention was riveted back on Grandfather. "Including a matched team of four for the carriage."

Yule and Sandy had ceased to breathe while Grandfather described the stakes of the wager. Of all Alex's cousins, those two were the most avid gamblers.

"So all we have to do is marry within the year?" Sandy's eyes had taken on a look of wonder.

"That is correct." Grandfather continued to look at Tom. "But you all must marry or none of you take the prize. No matter how many of you have already married."

"Damn." Francis's oath slipped out. He shook his head, crestfallen.

"What's wrong, Francis?" His twin nudged his arm, grinning. "Don't you think there's a lady out there who'll have you, even without a title?"

"More than would have you, Jules, even with a title." The brothers always disparaged one another, but their deep affection for each other assured the others they spoke only in jest.

"The question is, Tom," Grandfather turned his gaze back on his youngest grandson, "will you join your cousins, or will you rob them of their chance at happiness and financial security? Apparently, the choice is yours alone." He glanced around the cluster of eager faces. "I believe everyone else is in."

Every cousin nodded, their faces turned to stare pointedly at Tom.

"Damnation." Their youngest cousin ran a hand through his hair. "It's not fair, I tell you. You all got to sow your wild oats. Why can't I?"

"Oh, you can sow your oats aplenty for the next year, Tom." Sandy grinned at him. "You just have to have planted everything you want—and be married—by August 22nd of 1861." He moved to stand to the right of Tom while Yule flanked him on the left. "You don't want to be the only man-Jack of us who keeps the others from reaping the benefit of Grandfather's generosity, do you?"

"Just think how happy you'll make a dying man if you agree

to the wager." Julius patted Tom's arm, then squeezed it until the muscle bulged. "Think how unhappy the five of us will be if you don't."

"And think, Tom, you've got to marry sometime." Alex downed the rest of his drink and set the glass down. "You might as well make it count for something." Glancing around the room at his relatives' hostile faces, he shrugged. "Or the five of us can beat the ever-living tar out of you right now."

With a disgusted sigh, Tom pulled away from the threatening men surrounding him, went to stand in front of their grandfather, and peered up at the stoic elderly man. "I'll do it on one condition."

"And that is?" Grandfather glared down his nose, never a good sign.

"You buy me a ship of my own and finance me for the entire year." Looking as though he'd never budge an inch, Tom crossed his arms over his chest and met Grandfather's stare without a qualm. "If I must live all my bachelor days in a single year, by God, I want the ability to go where I please, when I please, and do what I please with whom I please instead of sailing for Father's company. With a ship of my own, I can captain her as I see fit."

"Done."

"What?" Tom looked dumbfounded. "Just like that? Without a shred of hesitation?"

"You thought I wouldn't assure your participation, my boy?" Grandfather shook his head, smiling all the while. "*Tsk, tsk*. You don't know me at all, do you, Tom?"

"Apparently not." Grumpy now he was trapped, Tom stalked over to the sideboard and poured himself another sizeable brandy. He tossed it down his throat then wiped his hand across his mouth. "I'll expect the ship within the month."

"Not unreasonable." Grandfather followed Tom and held out his glass. "I'll throw in the crew to boot."

"Damn right." Tom threw his glass into the fireplace, making the sparks fly, then poured a drink for his grandfather. "I'll be at my club until the ship is mine."

"Don't be angry, Tom." Alex draped his arm across his cousin's shoulder. "Just think of all the women you'll seduce with that sleek ship." He kissed his bunched fingers. "A veritable floating buffet of romance. And all yours—for a whole year."

"So it seems," Tom growled. "At least we can have a wager who'll be the first one wed." He gazed appraisingly at Alex. "You're the eldest, Alex. It should be you."

"I'll take that action." Yule stepped up to Julius. "Put me down for a hundred pounds that Alex is the first of us to marry."

"Done." Julius pulled a small, thick, black book and pencil from his inner jacket pocket and rifled through the pages. He turned to a new one, wrote down *Marriage Wagers*, then *First Wed*. "So, who wants some more of that wager?"

"I do." Alex pulled a small tablet out of his breast pocket, tore out a sheet, and scribbled on it. "There." He handed the sheet with his signature, a number, and the letters IOU on it. "If I'm to be a sacrificial lamb, I want to make something out of it to boot. Put me down to be married first and by the end of the month."

"But it's already the 22nd, Alex." Tom stared up at him, pole-axed. "How are you going to find a woman and get her to agree to marry you in less than ten days?"

"Very quickly, Tom." Alex laughed, although he had no clue how he was going to accomplish this feat. "Very quickly."

CHAPTER ONE

August, 1860
Hampshire, England

THE HEAT OF the day was coming on strong when the family landau swept up to the main walkway of Caxton Park, Alex's uncle's favorite country estate. The sprawling Tudor manor house was Alex's favorite as well. He never entered it without experiencing a sense of awe at the grandeur of the towering sandstone-walled edifice. Today was no different on that account. However, as Alex disembarked from the carriage, a shiver of anticipation shot down his spine. His greatest hope was that this house party would prove auspicious regarding his current endeavor: to find a wife.

He strolled down the gray stone walkway toward the main entrance of the house, the gravity of the wager he'd made with his grandfather and cousins weighing heavily on his mind. Boasting that he could court a young lady and convince her to marry him by the end of the month—now a mere week away—might not have been the best idea, but he'd wanted to make a bold move. Get the larger wager underway with a bit of a splash. He'd known on Wednesday he'd be coming to this house party, rather a card up his sleeve, so to speak. Now that he was here, however, the confidence that he could woo and wed so quickly began to wane.

Nonsense. Alex straightened his back, raised his chin, and continued to stride toward the front door, his scarlet uniform almost glowing in the bright sun. No reason at all why a young lady wouldn't want to marry him. Even though he'd been in the army for ten years and had lived rough and ready for much of it, he was a gentleman after all. He had sufficient income and family connections enough to recommend him. When the situation called for it, he could be quite charming—and this situation certainly called for it now. He'd been called handsome enough times to believe he wasn't repugnant to the fairer sex. Whenever he set his mind to something, it inevitably came to pass. So, if he desired a wife, then he'd bloody well get one this week.

He arrived at the front door and rapped on it smartly.

Drake, his uncle's longtime butler, opened the door, his face lighting with what passed for a smile from the staid servant.

"Captain Bancroft." The man bowed. "Lord Caxton has been awaiting your arrival. Will you join him in the library?"

"Certainly, Drake." Alex passed the man his hat and sword as he entered the house, glad to surrender them. "The footman has my trunk."

"Very good, sir. I will instruct him to put it in the Regent's Bedroom."

Alex's brows rose slightly. The Regent's Bedroom was usually reserved for the most important guests. Hitherto, he had always been housed in the small but serviceable Blue Room.

Drake motioned the footman through the entry hall toward the back of the house, then followed him.

Turning toward the library, Alex was about to leave the entry hall when his eye caught movement above him on the main staircase that wound gracefully up to the first floor of the manor. His gaze was drawn upward until it fell on a hooped skirt covered in white gauzy material with little pink flowers scattered capriciously all over it. The bell-like garment swayed charmingly as its wearer stopped, waiting her turn to descend the stairs.

Alex's gaze rose further to the face of the young lady as she looked over the railing to admire a family portrait on the opposite wall. She had an arresting face, oval and fashionably pale, framed by rich chestnut hair styled in long ringlets that bounced when she shook her head. This charming action took place often as she talked to her companion. Her full pink lips drew a sigh from Alex, who wondered what it might be like to kiss that perfect bow of a mouth. Past caring about the conventions, he frankly stared at her, entranced. She spoke and laughed with a smaller brunette lady, who was quite well and good, but who couldn't hold a candle to her enchanting companion, who seemed to have stepped out of a fashion plate.

"You'd best close your mouth before you start catching flies, Alex." His cousin Yule's voice brought him out of his musings about the mysterious young lady.

About to retort in the negative, Alex stopped when he had to close his open mouth to form the words. Had he been gawking *that* badly? Turning quickly toward Yule, he smiled broadly. "That's not all I wager I'll catch this weekend, cousin. What brings you to Hampshire?"

"The same as you, I'd say." Yule scanned the crowds of guests standing about chatting. "To catch the eye of some delectable young lady." Taller than Alex by an inch, Yule craned his neck back as he perused the ladies standing on the stairs, waiting to follow the throng descending to the ground floor. "Although I daresay you have a bit of an advantage over me by wearing your regimentals. Ladies do love a man in uniform."

"You are not wrong in that, cousin." Alex chuckled, his gaze still resting on the young lady in pink. There was something about her, perhaps her perfect English maiden look, but perhaps something more than that compelled his continued gaze. "At least I hope you aren't."

At that moment, the lady in pink glanced over the balustrade down at the milling throng in the foyer as if searching for something or someone. Just as quickly, she looked away, but her head snapped back toward the lower hall, her gaze riveted on Alex. Her eyes widened—with recognition? It couldn't be. He'd certainly remember this lady had they been introduced. Had she mistaken him for someone else?

"Yule…Yule." His cousin had begun a conversation with another acquaintance, but Alex had to discover this lady's name. "Yule!"

"What is it, Alexander, that makes you so vilely rude?" The annoyance in his cousin's voice was almost palpable.

"That lady on the landing there." Alex couldn't point—even his excitement wouldn't allow him to be that impolite—but he nodded in the general direction.

"There are at least six young ladies on the landing." Yule's stiffened stance and thinned lips showed his displeasure with Alex.

"The one in the pink-flowered dress. Do you know who she is?"

Yule glanced upward, then shook his head. "Never seen her before." He took a second look and a smile spread over his face. "Although I can see why you'd be interested in an introduction. Quite fetching, isn't she?"

"Indeed." Alex continued to stare, almost afraid to take his eyes off her. The young lady in question had turned back to her companion, but every so often shot a look at him, as if to assure herself he was still there. "But how am I to meet her?"

"I assume since your uncle invited her here, he or his wife must know her." Yule's impatience seemed to be growing. "I suggest you find him and beg an introduction."

"Absolute genius, old chap." Alex slapped Yule on the back, then hurried past him into the library. Why hadn't he thought of Uncle Jack? Too addlepated by the young lady's presence, obviously. He hurried into the library, then scanned the room.

He easily spotted his uncle, Lord Caxton, standing next to his wife Lucinda, an American lady he'd met and married during his trip to New York last year. She was a very sweet woman, willowy with a delicate air, yet vivacious—and close to twenty years his uncle's junior. Despite the vast age difference, the pair seemed to have genuine affection for one another, and Alex had sincerely wished them happy on their return to England last autumn.

"Uncle Jack." Alex wormed his way through the packed room until he stood in front of his uncle and aunt in front of the fireplace. "Good afternoon, uncle. Good afternoon, Aunt Lucinda. Thank you so much for inviting me to your house party." He bowed formally. "It's good to see you both again."

"Never stand on ceremony with me, my boy." Uncle Jack grabbed Alex up in a hug then pounded him on the back. At almost fifty, his uncle was still a bear of a man: tall, barrel-chested, and strong of arm, though now silver-haired. Nothing at all like his brother, Alex's father, had been, though there had been a family likeness in their faces. "Now that's a real howdy-do." His uncle had picked up several American speech peculiarities while he'd been across the pond that Alex found bewildering. "Glad to have you here again, nephew."

"I am happy to be here, uncle." He turned to his aunt's eager, smiling face. "And you are looking particularly fetching today, aunt. Having guests must agree with you."

"I suppose it does, Alex, although I've done nothing much but give instructions to the servants." She blushed and cast her gaze to the floor. "Jack wouldn't let me lift a finger to help with anything."

"That I would not, my dear." His uncle gazed fondly at his wife, then stepped close to Alex and whispered, "No one knows yet, but Lucinda is in *a delicate condition.*"

Alex jerked backward, his face heating a trifle. Of course, he understood the meaning of that phrase, but he'd rarely known any genteel woman in such a condition. He supposed he should be as matter of fact about it as he was with the camp followers of his unit who never sought to hide their pregnancies. But, somehow, with his aunt's situation, he couldn't help but be embarrassed. And surprised she was still out and about in public.

"This party is my last appearance, Alex." Almost as though she'd read his mind, Lucinda's soft voice brought him out of his musings. "I hope we haven't shocked you."

"Not at all, aunt. My best wishes for you both." Alex managed to smile, although just knowing her condition made him feel scandalous. Perhaps he should change the subject before things got even more uncomfortable. "I came to find you to ask your help with a small matter."

"My help?" Lucinda's delicate brows shot up. "What can I help you with?"

"Well, either you or my uncle." Hesitant now that the time had come, Alex cleared his throat a couple of times and took a deep breath. "There's a young lady here to whom I should like to be introduced."

A sweet smile spread across his aunt's face while his uncle let out a laugh that turned all heads in the room toward them. "I told you, my dear." His uncle puffed out his chest. "I told you he'd be out to win that wager while he was here."

Inwardly, Alex groaned. Not that he'd thought his grandfather's wager would be kept a secret—he was too worldly to ever believe that. He had hoped, however, that his own wager to be the first one wed could be kept *sub rosa*. Certainly no young lady hearing of it would give him a second thought. "So you've heard about that, uncle?"

"I had luncheon with your grandfather yesterday."

That would explain it. "I do hope no one else knows of it." Alex sent a silent plea to God. "I think it might hinder my hopes of success."

Chuckling, Uncle Jack nodded. "Never fear, m' boy. Mum's the word for me and Lucinda. Right, m'dear?"

"Of course, my dear." Her light brown eyes were merry. "I promise we will do whatever we can to assist you in your suit, Alex." She took his arm. "So you must tell us who this young lady is to whom you wish to be introduced."

MISS EMMA WASHER had to admit she was glad she'd accepted Lady Caxton's invitation to her house party, even though Emma knew only a handful of the people here. Of course, Lady Tilney, her social sponsor, had insisted she attend, so she was happy it had turned into a pleasant experience.

"Despite your recent circumstances, my dear, you really must begin to move in society if you are to meet eligible gentlemen. Your first duty, you understand, is to marry and, if I am to do right by you, marry well." Lady Tilney nodded sharply as she'd written to Lady Caxton, accepting the invitation and giving Emma no opportunity to protest. "My daughter Augusta and I will accompany you, and between the both of us, perhaps you'll enjoy yourself *and* find a husband."

A distant cousin of Emma's late aunt, Lady Tilney had taken on Emma in June when the current Season had been all but over. Unused to English society, Emma had hoped she'd not have to go out in public at all, but Lady Tilney had managed to coax her out twice. During those two wretched entertainments, Emma had stubbornly maintained her status as a wallflower until Lady Tilney had thrown up her hands in defeat.

Emma had been grateful when the Season had ended and her sponsor had ceased her incessant attempts to put her about in London. The woman truly meant well, even if she didn't understand Emma's reluctance. Her official time of mourning for her aunt was long past, yet due to the horrific circumstances of her aunt's death, Emma didn't seem able to put her grief aside. After some coaxing from Lady Tilney's elder daughter Augusta, Emma agreed to make up for her poor performance at Lady Ripley's ball and Almack's by agreeing to attend the house party in Hampshire.

Now that she was here, Emma's spirits actually seemed to take a turn upward. Oh, she'd only been here not quite a day, but the weather was glorious, there was a garden she'd discovered last evening and strolled in twice, and the people around her had been extraordinarily kind. Augusta had just fetched her for another walk before luncheon and Emma had enthusiastically joined her. Lively chatter surrounding them made such a difference in her mood. Perhaps this weekend would be enjoyable after all. She glanced over the railing at the throng of new guests entering the manor house. Who knew, but she might find one of the few acquaintances she'd made in London also attending the house party.

"The gown Lady Caxton was wearing at breakfast was so very pretty, don't you think, Emma?" Augusta Hardy loved nothing as much as the most up-to-date fashion. "That shade of pale green is a becoming color for her, although most blondes can't manage it. The cut was pleasing as well. Not too much decolletage yet alluring all the same. Oh, bother."

The quick glance took in the group of people below before Augusta's exclamation brought Emma's attention back to her friend. "What—"

No, wait. What had she just seen? Emma jerked her head back to the mass of moving guests down below. Yes, yes it was. Eyes widening, she stared down at the gentleman dressed in the brilliant scarlet of the British Regimental uniform. An indescribable wave of happiness rolled over her, giving her a feeling of satisfaction she'd not had in many months. How wonderful to find a British officer here of all places. She turned back to Augusta, who had not stopped talking all the while.

"Now I shall have to go change again."

"I beg your pardon?" Emma glanced back over the balustrade, but the officer continued to stand there staring upward.

"Look here." Augusta presented her arm to Emma. The frothy lace on her right sleeve had come loose and dangled most unbecomingly onto her arm.

"Oh, dear. Yes, you must go back and have Marks attend to it." Another quick look, but the scarlet-clad officer continued to stare up…good lord, was he looking at her?

"Exactly. I'm sorry we won't have time for our walk before luncheon, my dear." Her friend had turned to go back upstairs.

One more peep over the railing at the handsome gentleman decided Emma. "I believe I am strong enough to venture out into the garden by myself, Augusta. I think it would be good for me to start going about on my own occasionally." She leaned toward her friend, hoping to convince her. "Your mother will be so pleased to hear about my solitary stroll."

Augusta pursed her lips, then touched the lace again and nodded. "Very well. If Marks can repair it quickly, I'll join you out in the garden."

"I'll be looking for you." Emma hoped she sounded sincere, although she'd prefer it if the person joining her in the garden was a certain officer standing downstairs.

Hoisting her skirts, her friend hurried back up the stairs, and Emma breathed a sigh of relief. Surreptitiously, she touched her hair, hoping it was still neatly coiffed, and turned to look over the railing again only to find the handsome young officer vanished.

"Drat!" Giving a great sigh, Emma held up her skirts and swiftly descended the rest of the stairs. Obviously another guest of Lord and Lady Caxton, the officer couldn't have gone far, although if he'd just arrived, he might have gone to his room to freshen up. Except all the bedrooms were upstairs and he had certainly not passed her on the staircase. Had he gone out to the garden? Tempting idea, but Emma shook her head. What was the first thing a good guest did upon arrival? Greet his host and hostess.

Standing in the midst of the entry hall, Emma gazed first one way then the other. She'd no idea where Lord and Lady Caxton were receiving their guests. To the left was the entrance to the library, to the right, a reception room. With so many guests milling about, there was no way to tell. She could ask someone where the earl was, but it wasn't proper to speak to someone to whom one had not been introduced.

A footman carrying a tray of cups containing lemonade passed by her, expertly weaving his way among the guests. Emma breathed a sigh of relief. Servants she knew how to deal with. She reached for a glass and the footman stopped. "Can you tell me where I might find Lord Caxton?"

"In the library, miss." He nodded to her then continued on his way.

Emma took a sip of the lemonade then set it on a tray sitting out of the way on a carved teak sideboard and set out once more. Holding her shoulders back, she raised her chin and sallied forth, down the short corridor and into the library.

The small room was packed with guests, so tightly, in fact, Emma's skirts wedged between two gentlemen conversing on her right and a rather large lady directly in her way. Pressing her hoops inward, she managed to free herself and finally gazed around the room, searching for a glimpse of Lord or Lady Caxton. She wasn't short, but the guests were so thick she had to raise herself up on tiptoe to look for the couple. At last, two ladies brushed past her, heading out of the stifling space. Emma bounded forward into the empty space then stopped short.

Before her stood Lord and Lady Caxton, smiling and conversing with the very handsome British officer she'd seen in the entry hall. So surprised she couldn't think what to say, Emma instead took in the officer head to toe. This close she could see just how handsome he really was, and not just from the allure of his regimentals. Taller than she by almost a head, the gentleman had dark blue eyes framed by sooty black lashes that had widened as much as her own, she believed. His uniform set off his physique to perfection, accentuating his broad shoulders and neat waist. At last, her gaze came to rest on the firm lips that had quickly turned up in a wide smile.

"Now this is a stroke of luck, eh, my dear?" Lord Caxton beamed at his wife. "Instead of Mohammed going to the mountain, the mountain's come to Mohammed."

"I beg pardon, my lord?" Emma frowned, then quickly adjusted her face into more graceful lines.

"He means I was just coming to find you, my dear." Lady Caxton took her arm and guided her toward the officer. Emma's heart took off racing, as though she'd run a long way trying to find some sort of haven. "This gentleman has asked for an introduction to the charming young lady he saw descending the stairs. He described her in such detail, I knew it could be no one but you." The countess squeezed her arm gently. "May I, my dear?"

Overwhelmed, Emma gazed up at the officer and could only nod.

"Miss Washer, may I introduce Captain Alexander Bancroft, Lord Caxton's nephew. Alex, this is Miss Emma Washer. Lady Tilney acted as her Social sponsor this past Season."

Captain Bancroft's deep blue eyes, gazing at her steadfastly, seemed to pierce her soul with happiness. She smiled back at him, exuding every ounce of joy she possessed. "I am truly glad to meet you, Captain." The mantle of protection she'd so longed for seemed suddenly within her grasp, making her words deeply heartfelt. "So very, truly glad to meet you."

CHAPTER TWO

"AS I AM to meet you, Miss Washer." He seized her hand and kissed it, the warmth of her skin emanating through her glove. "I saw you just now on the stairs and immediately begged my aunt for the introduction. I am amazed we have not met before now."

"Miss Washer has only recently graced London society with her presence." Uncle Jack beamed at them. "She arrived not two months ago, isn't that right, my dear?"

"Yes, it is, my lord." Miss Washer cast her gaze downward very demurely. "Lady Tilney brought me out last June. She was kind enough to ask Lady Caxton for an invitation to this house party." With suddenness, the lady raised her head, her eyes gazing deeply into Alex's. "I am so very grateful to her for doing so."

The penetrating blue of those eyes, the long lacy lashes framing them, sent a stab of hunger to Alex's gut. "As am I, Miss Washer." He turned a grin on his aunt. "You have my sincere thanks as well, Aunt Lucinda. I should have hated to have to wait until next spring to welcome Miss Washer back to England."

"Then I suggest you make the most of this meeting and escort the young lady out to the rose garden, my boy." His uncle had no claim to subtlety. "The heat shouldn't bother you a'tall." He chuckled. "I daresay it might even speed things along."

No subtlety whatsoever.

Alex cleared his throat. "Would you like to accompany me to the rose garden, Miss Washer?" He shot a warning look at his uncle. "Or perhaps a stroll to the Great Folly? It and the small park surrounding it were devised by a very famous landscape gardener."

Miss Washer's face lit up. "I have visited the rose garden twice since yesterday, Captain Bancroft, and it is indeed a lovely spot. However, I would certainly enjoy a visit to the folly as I have not yet seen it."

"Splendid." Alex offered his arm, which Miss Washer took with a smile. "Thank you, uncle and aunt. We will return in good time for dinner."

"Well, I should hope so, my boy. I don't know what you could find to do out at the folly for three hours." His uncle snorted. "Or perhaps I do. Enjoy yourselves."

Alex moved them quickly toward the doorway, praying for no other comment from his relative.

As a lady should, Miss Washer seemed to not have heard such a ribald comment and serenely kept up with his quickened pace as they left the library, turned right, and came out on the southern side of the manor house. Alex gave a silent sigh of relief and they set off across the lawn, making for a crushed stone path that led to the folly.

"You are enjoying your stay here at Caxton Park so far, Miss Washer?" Not a stunning conversational gambit to open with, but Alex didn't wish for a silent walk. If he really had it in mind to court and marry Miss Washer in such a short time, he needed to find out as much about her as possible, and quickly.

"I am, Captain. Everyone has been extraordinarily kind to me. Lord and Lady Caxton, especially." The lady smiled broadly, bringing out a small dimple in her left cheek he hadn't noticed before. "I'm not used to all the hubbub of crowds, and was a bit reticent at dinner last evening, but they've made certain I've been well taken care of and made to feel welcome."

"They are two of the dearest people, I must say." Alex smiled in return, still entranced by the memory of that dimple. "I was often a guest here when my uncle was still a bachelor. He's very serious about maintaining the family connection. After my father died, my uncle insisted my mother and I come here for our mourning period, so we could all condole together. He said since I was then his heir, it was only right for me to feel as though Caxton Park was my home."

Alex nodded to the vista before them. He did think of it as his home. The parkland they were walking through gave way to a magnificent stand of oak trees about a mile to their left. To the right, on the other side of the manor house, lay a large pond ringed with bracken and cattails that boasted a bounty of fish, stocked by his uncle every year. They had fished there many a time together. His uncle's hospitality had always been generous to a fault.

"You must be very dear to him indeed." The lady walked in silence beside him for a moment. "Do you reside here all the time?"

"Hardly at all, I fear. My duties to queen and country keep me from it for much of the year." Alex shook his head. As his uncle was growing older, he wished he could stay at Caxton Park more often. "I do get some time here and there, like this house party, and a few days at Christmas, but recently I've been quartered in London, awaiting the next posting for the regiment."

Miss Washer gripped his arm then relaxed. "Her Majesty's Army does such important work. I am always grateful for their presence around the world, keeping us all safe." She peered up at him. "Will you miss it very much when you have to resign your commission?"

Alex stopped dead.

Miss Washer turned to him, her face bewildered. "What is wrong, Captain?"

"Why ever would you think I would resign my commission, Miss Washer?" Appalled, Alex could only stare at the woman, as shocked as though she had grown two heads. Never had he even considered leaving the army.

"When you inherit your uncle's title, won't you be expected to resign?" The lady looked totally confused. "I've known of several officers who did so."

With a chuckle, Alex relaxed and resumed their stroll. "Yes, you are correct in that. Most gentlemen who inherit do resign their commissions as their duties then shift from protecting the country to being part of the country we protect. In my case, however, I don't believe I shall be my uncle's heir for very much longer."

"Why not?"

About to open his mouth to explain the circumstances, Alex caught himself. He certainly could not divulge the secret his uncle and aunt had entrusted to him. Especially as such a topic could not be broached with an innocent young lady such as Miss Washer. But he could give her a hint. "My uncle is newly married. When he announced his intention to wed last year, I naturally assumed that I would eventually be superseded by his own offspring."

"I see." She walked on, a thoughtful look on her face. "Are you sorry you may not inherit the title?"

"On the contrary." Alex laughed and patted her hand. "I am completely relieved. I never expected to inherit the Caxton title and am truly thankful it likely will pass me by. When I bought my commission, I knew my true calling was the army. There is nothing I love better than being part of the regiment. Giving my all for queen and country is the best sort of life I believe I can live. The sense of honor I get when I think of fulfilling that sacred duty is beyond compare." The magnitude of the moment stole Alex's breath. He'd always been passionate about serving his country. The depths of his passion, however, always surprised him. "I can't think of anything else I'd rather do with my life."

"Such dedication to service makes you well suited to that life then." Miss Washer's approval gave Alex a moment of pride. "It's good to enjoy what you do for a living."

"That is certainly true. I've known some gentlemen who entered professions to which they were ill-suited, thinking only of the substantial wages they would earn." Alex shook his head. Poor rotters. "They never found much happiness in life that I saw."

This conversation needed to shift directions if he was to discover more about Miss Washer. "But we are taking too serious a turn, I think. Here we are at the folly and I insist we find a better topic."

Giggling, Miss Washer released his arm and ran up the steps of the small round edifice. "Then you must tell me about the folly. I haven't seen one at all here." She entered the building, gazed up at the rounded roof, turned in a circle. "Hello!" Delighted with the slight echo, she laughed again and called out louder, "Helloooo!"

Enjoying the charming sight, Alex stood back, watching her play.

A bevy of doves that had been roosting in the structure took flight, flapping frantically until they winged out of the folly. Alex feared they might have startled Miss Washer, but she continued to laugh and explore the small building. "When was the folly constructed?"

"In the 18th Century." Alex mounted the four steps to stand at the building's entrance. "It was erected by Capability Brown. You've heard of him?"

She shook her head and adjusted her silk shawl over her shoulders, as though the marble walls had given off a slight chill. "Was he very famous?"

"Yes, he was. Many people seek an invitation here just to come visit the folly because he built it." Gazing at Miss Washer, her cheeks pink, her eyes sparkling with delight, Alex was once more enchanted by her loveliness. The idea of formally courting her excited him to no end. Why no one had asked for her hand already astonished him. "I am curious, Miss Washer, why we have not met before this? You have been out in Society only recently, my uncle said?"

Some of the brightness in her face dimmed, but she smiled as she came closer to him. "I have only been in England for two months, Captain. Before that I spent some time with my aunt and uncle in the Orient."

"Really?" This was interesting news indeed. "I must admit to being somewhat jealous of you then, Miss Washer. I have hoped for some time that my regiment would be sent to India or Pakistan, to continue keeping the peace in those countries. So far, I have only been sent as far as the Crimea."

"You were?" Eagerness flooded Miss Washer's face. She leaned toward him, asking in hushed tones, "Were you part of the charge of the Light Brigade?"

Alex had gotten that question many times before this, so he merely smiled and shook his head. "I'm part of the infantry, not the cavalry, so although I took part in the Battle of Balaclava, I had no part in the charge itself. You've read Lord Tennyson's poem, I take it?"

"Yes, I have." She looked at him, starry-eyed. "How absolutely stirring it was, although I expect the actual event was much more violent than the poem suggests."

"In that you are correct, Miss Washer. Shall we start back to the house?" Lord, he didn't want to talk about that bloody, awful battle. He'd tried to turn the conversation, but the lady seemed to bring it back to less palatable subjects. "I see there are other guests on their way here. Soon the folly will be absolutely teeming with people. The problem with small buildings, you know."

"It does seem difficult to find a place where we can talk uninterrupted." Miss Washer puckered her brow. "Can we sit there, on that little bench by the path? As long as we're in sight of everyone, I'm certain there can be no harm in conversing together." She smiled up at him, and he caught his breath at the longing in her eyes. "I so wish to hear all about your service in the

Crimea." Her liquid blue eyes cast a spell on him. "Won't you tell me about it?"

How on earth could he bear to disappoint her? Alex motioned to the bench, dappled in sunlight, sitting there as if waiting for them.

Miss Washer eagerly sank down onto it, pulling her shawl well over her shoulders and arms. "Now tell me first, Captain Bancroft, what is the Crimea like?"

Drawing a deep breath, Alex launched into a detailed description of the area around the Alma River. "The 30th Regiment of Foot under the command of Major General Sir George Cathcart arrived in the Crimea in September of 1854. The area we occupied was the bank of the Alma River, a rather picturesque site when troops aren't roiling in the water or bombarding the embankments. The water was broad and shallow there, and very clear. You could count every stone on the bottom if you'd had time. Tall cypress trees lined some of the edges of the banks, although by the time the battle had ended, there wasn't much left of the flora."

The smile never left Miss Washer's lips. "My goodness, Captain, you make it sound idyllic."

"It was until the shooting began."

"Your regiment was part of that action?"

Sighing, Alex shook his head. "Unfortunately, no. My regiment—my whole division, in fact—wasn't engaged in that battle."

Some of the light went out of Miss Washer's face.

"But we made up for it at Balaclava."

"Tell me." Miss Washer leaned toward him, now hanging on his every word.

Chest swelling with pride, Alex dove into the tale, leaving out the most harrowing details in deference to the lady's delicate sensibilities. He did, however, manage to convey the regiment's valiant efforts that supported the cavalry and the highland regiments. "So you see, Miss Washer, while we weren't at the charge that Lord Tennyson described so vividly, we supported the cavalry in every way possible, both before and after that action."

"You make me faint with pride, Captain Bancroft." Miss Washer gazed up at him, her eyes dewy with unshed tears. "Our brave men in uniform have made all the difference to so many thousands of British citizens the world over, providing protection to us all to keep us free from harm. I am so pleased and proud to know you and be able to thank you for your service."

"Thank you, Miss Washer." Her sincere admiration touched a chord deep within him. He rarely thought about the repercussions of his occupation to singular citizens. On the battlefield, he thought only of the immediate objective, and afterward, of the war's larger purpose. Now this lady, who he scarcely knew, had made him catch a glimpse of the far-reaching effects his efforts on those distant foreign battlegrounds provided to those at home. "I am humbled by your praise. My duty has always been given with queen and country as a whole in mind, not individuals such as yourself. I shall henceforth reflect on the fact that each British man, woman, and child is my responsibility to keep safe whether they are foreign nationals or inhabitants of the farthest hamlet in Cornwall."

"Then I am thrilled to have made that small contribution, Captain." She clasped her hands before her bosom, bringing them immediately to his attention. Miss Washer had a figure to rival any actress on today's stage.

He really must find out more about her. With determination, he rose and offered his arm. "I think we should repair to the house now, Miss Washer. The sun is full hot and I am afraid you may feel the effects of it if we tarry here longer."

"Yes, indeed, Captain. You are very thoughtful." She stood and took his arm, as naturally as though she'd been doing it all her life. "I was being silly. I should have brought my parasol, then I could have been treated to more stirring tales of war."

With a smile, Alex started them back toward the house. "Perhaps we can continue our conversation in the drawing room after dinner."

"That would be lovely, Captain Bancroft." The sweet smile on her lips sent a pang of longing to his groin. Pretty, sweet, and attentive, Miss Washer had become a most dear acquaintance in an amazingly short span of time. If things continued to progress at this accelerated pace, he might very well be a married man by the time the house party was over.

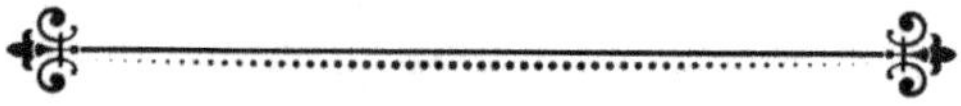

CHAPTER THREE

IMPATIENT AS THE gentlemen lingered after dinner with their port and cigars, Alex ended up pacing about the smoking room, to which they had removed. He'd been unable to sit with Miss Washer at dinner—they'd been separated by almost the length of the dining table—so now he jealously counted the minutes they must continue to remain apart due to the need for his uncle to smoke like the proverbial chimney. Alex gulped the remaining port in his glass and splashed in another hefty tot. There were so many gentlemen in the party they very well might not join the ladies until midnight. A fate he'd give much to escape. Miss Washer's company this afternoon had been most pleasant, and he was eager to continue their conversation, especially if he could engage her to talk about herself. Flattering, of course, that she was so interested in him and his life, but dash it all, he'd like to know something about her other than her name if he was seriously considering marrying her.

"Are you about to break ranks and join the ladies on your own, Alex?" Uncle Jack's voice rose above the din of the others.

"Of course not, uncle." Alex straightened and peered through the fog of smoke toward the place his uncle's voice seemed to come from.

"Then why the devil are you hanging about the door?"

Alex glanced over his shoulder and, sure enough, the door to the corridor was directly behind him. "I guess I just fetched up here." He shrugged. "The room is rather crowded."

"It is, I can't deny it." Uncle Jack rose and strode toward him. "I'll have to designate a larger chamber for the smoking room after this." His face brightened. "Which means I'll be able to put my hand into the decoration of it. This was originally a study and I didn't really do much when I decided it should be my smoking room except have the velvet drapes installed." His gaze wandered around the room. "Perhaps an Egyptian theme, eh?" He waved his cigar. "Egyptian tobacco, you know."

"A delightful idea, Lord Caxton." Lord Braeton had joined them, a young lord Alex had met before and liked quite a lot. "Will you journey to Egypt to secure authentic pieces for the room?"

Inwardly, Alex groaned. Get his uncle started on his previous trip to Egypt and the evening was lost.

"Already got 'em, Braeton. Took a trip there in '42, brought back all manner of statues, furniture, and the like. Stored up in the attics somewhere. I'll take you there…"

Alex's face must have given away his dismay, for his uncle gave out a great laugh and clapped him on the back. "Another time, Braeton. My nephew is impatient to join the ladies. Gentlemen, if you will finish your port and extinguish your cigars, we'll head to the drawing room. There's a dish of peppermints by the door for those who wish to assure they have pleasing breaths for the fairer sex."

Not a bad idea, that. Even though he didn't smoke, Alex grabbed a peppermint from the footman's basket and popped it into his mouth. One never knew when a lady's sensibility would need to be appeased.

They proceeded down the corridor, up the stairs, and into the drawing room. During their march, Alex had hung back until he was about midway down the procession. No need to seem as eager as he felt. As soon as he entered the room, however, his gaze darted quickly around the pleasant chamber, decorated in a more feminine scheme of pink and green, searching for Miss Washer. He discovered her, teacup in hand, standing by the banked fireplace, and immediately headed toward her.

"Ah, Miss Washer, I can scarcely contain my excitement at finally being able to speak with you once more." Alex bowed, smiling broadly. "Dinner may have been delicious, but it would have been much better had we not been so far removed from one another."

"I believe I must agree with that sentiment, Captain Bancroft." She lifted her face to his, her intriguingly blue eyes gazing deeply into his. "I fear my lack of status will keep us apart during meals here."

"I could speak to my aunt and uncle about that." He'd contemplated that during dinner, in fact. "Ask for at least one evening when we may sit where we choose."

"That would be wonderful." Miss Washer nodded toward the sideboard where several teapots, cups, and saucers sat. "Would you like some tea?"

"Yes, I think I shall." Alex started toward the table, fully intending to pour his own, but Miss Washer quickened her pace and arrived first.

"Allow me, Captain." She set her cup down, picked up another in that hand and a teapot with the other, and poured very prettily.

He could get used to seeing that sight each morning and evening.

"Milk and sugar?" Her voice lilted upward and a streak of heat shot through Alex's body, lodging squarely in his groin.

"Yes, please," he said breathlessly.

She smiled up at him as she plopped two lumps of sugar into the cup and added a splash of milk. "Shall we sit and continue our conversation from this afternoon? I'm certain you have much more to tell me about your time in the Crimea."

Nodding, he led her to an isolated grouping of a Queen Anne chair and chaise near the French windows that gave onto the back gardens. The perfect place for a confidential conversation. Miss Washer sat squarely in the middle of the green jacquard chaise, leaving him the chair. Once he was seated, he sipped his tea, which was excellently done, and leaned toward the lady. "Please allow me to inquire about you, Miss Washer. We seemed to have spoken only about me this afternoon, and I am eager to discover as much about you as you have about me. You are a lady of mystery to me at present."

To his consternation, her eyes grew wide, she appeared to stiffen, and grasped her teacup in a vise-like grip. What the devil was the matter with his simple request?

EMMA HAD KNOWN he would want to learn more about her. Had dreaded it, in fact. She'd also known there was no way to escape giving Captain Bancroft at least some information about her circumstances. The little bits of conversation she'd practiced aloud in her room this afternoon rose immediately to her lips. She could only pray they would be enough. "What would you like to know, Captain?"

"Well, I suppose I would like to know of your family." He nodded toward the manor house. "You have the advantage of knowing quite a bit about mine by now."

Relieved, she smiled broadly. That one was easy. "I am the daughter of Mr. Josiah Washer and his wife, Emmaline. I grew up in Lyme Regis where my father was a solicitor."

"That is a lovely seaside town, Miss Washer. I visited it some years ago and found it delightful." Captain Bancroft's approval was gratifying. Emma wished the tale of her family life began and ended in the peaceful town where she'd been born. That, however, wasn't the case.

"It was a wonderful place to grow up, Captain." She shook her head and smiled sadly. "Unfortunately, I lived there only twelve years. My parents succumbed to an outbreak of typhoid, and I was sent to live with my aunt and uncle Washer."

"Oh, I'm so sorry for your loss, Miss Washer." The captain's mouth thinned, and he glanced around the room as though he didn't know where to look.

"Thank you, Captain, but you needn't be discomfited." The last thing she wanted to do was move them into a fit of melancholy. "It happened above ten years ago. And at least I had that brief idyllic time with my parents. Not every child does, you know."

"That is true." He gave her a brief smile. "You will always have those precious memories."

If only they were the sole memories she possessed.

"So you now live with your aunt and uncle?" Captain Bancroft sipped his tea, his gaze on her. "I thought someone else sponsored you this past Season."

Fighting down the urge to panic, Emma sipped her tea as well and launched into the story she'd decided to tell him. "My aunt and uncle have not been out in Society much. They had no children and my uncle was a shareholder in the East India Company so they spent a great deal of their lives out in India. Lady Tilney, a dear friend of my aunt, agreed to bring me out." And that was as much as she was prepared to tell Captain Bancroft about herself for the moment. Before he could reply, Emma set her teacup on the table and rose. "Would you mind escorting me outside for a breath of fresh air, Captain? The drawing room seems overly warm suddenly."

"Of course, Miss Washer." A look of pleasure came over his face as he set his cup aside and came to his feet. He offered his red-clad arm and a little chill ran up her spine as she took it. "Nothing could give me more pleasure."

Well, she'd see about that. Resisting the urge to cling to that strong arm, Emma tossed her head and laughed. She glanced over at Lady Caxton, in deep conversation with Lady Hunstanton. If they slipped out quickly, perhaps no one would notice their absence. "I am happy we are in accord once more."

He led her to the French windows and, with a strange little flutter in her stomach, Emma followed him outside onto the veranda.

The night air was soft and warm with a slight breeze that brought the faint scent of roses wafting from the nearby garden. Oil lamps suspended from the ceiling of the veranda at perfect intervals provided a gentle glow while still allowing for a shadowy, romantic atmosphere. The perfect setting to further her acquaintance with the captain.

They slowed to a stop halfway between the lamps, in enough shadow that Emma need not fear Captain Bancroft could see her face. Her cheeks were already hot from the knowledge of what she intended to do. Turning to gaze out over the manicured lawn, Emma released her grip on his arm and leaned against the railing. "It's such a lovely night, isn't it?"

"The loveliest one I've ever seen."

The strange timbre of his voice made her jerk her head toward him. He wasn't looking out at the darkened vista she'd been peering at. His gaze rested squarely on her.

Emma's heart beat so hard against her breast she feared he could hear it. But she couldn't dwell on that. This was the chance she'd hoped for. She swayed toward him, tilting her head back so she looked directly into his eyes. "Shall we make it even better, Captain?"

Seeming much darker than their normal blue, his eyes widened, then his head lowered until his lips rested against her ear. "Are you merely flirting with me, Miss Washer, or was that an honest invitation to a kiss?"

"Oh, I am an honest woman, Captain Bancroft." She licked her lips then pursed them. "Do you doubt it?"

"Not at all." He brushed a stray lock of her hair back off her forehead, winding it slowly around the shell of her ear, sending chills down her whole body. "However, I wouldn't wish to persuade myself that my own desires were the same as yours if they were not."

Trembling with anticipation, Emma swayed closer to him. "And what are your desires, Captain?" Her words, throaty and breathless, came out a bare whisper.

His lips now hovered scarcely above hers. "To kiss you, of course."

"Then our desires are indeed in accord." She held her breath as he plunged his lips onto hers.

Emma had never kissed a man before, hadn't been completely certain she'd be able to entice the captain to do it. Her only experience with the intimate act had been secondhand, surreptitiously watching a couple kissing onboard the *Scotia* on her return trip to England. Miss Mills and Mr. Huckabee had been extremely enthusiastic and had seemed to enjoy their encounter so much Emma had secretly longed to have that experience as well.

The fervor of his kiss caught her by surprise, however. Never had she imagined it would feel like this. The pressure of his mouth against hers—lips both soft and firm at the same time—sent a fiery jolt throughout her body. Her cheeks heated until her head felt as though an inferno raged there. Suddenly, her knees seemed weak as water, threatening to collapse her to the ground. She put a hand on his chest to steady herself, eager to continue even though her head began to spin. He must have thought she meant to push him away, for he leaned backward, trying to break the kiss.

Emma would have none of that. This sensation of warmth, of comfort, of safety was too good to lose. She grasped his jacket and pulled him back to her. That action must have convinced him, for he cradled her head in his hands, turning her face until their lips fit together perfectly. She relaxed in his arms, determined to enjoy every second of the kiss: their incredible closeness, the scent of citrus he wore, the flutter of butterflies all through her stomach that made her wish to never stop.

Aroused by these heady sensations, Emma could have stood there kissing Captain Bancroft forever, except now there seemed to be a new sort of pressure on her mouth. The captain was pressing something against the seam of her closed lips. Glorying in the moment, Emma couldn't think what he was trying to do. She felt so incredibly safe and warm and happy she could only press back against his lips, wishing to convey her joy in their closeness. She'd been attracted to the captain from the first, but she'd never imagined she'd feel this rush of happiness, especially toward a man who was almost a stranger. If only it would never end.

He pushed a little harder at her lips and she started to open her mouth, wondering if that was what he wanted her to do. But when she gave in that tiny bit, with an audible groan, he thrust his tongue into her mouth.

Shocked to her core, Emma emitted a shriek and jerked backward, pulling her body and mouth away from him. She clamped her hand over her lips, not at all certain what had just happened. When she could think again, she glared up at Captain Bancroft, who stood trying not to smile at her. "What did you think you were doing, sir?"

"I thought I was kissing a very willing young lady, Miss Washer. You assured me you were before we began." The wretch didn't even try to sound repentant.

"That was not kissing...not that last part at the end." Miss Mills and Mr. Huckabee had not looked as though they were doing anything at all like that.

"Oh, I assure you, it was." He cocked his head, looking curious. "No gentleman has ever deepened a kiss with you before?"

Emma gave thanks for the thick shadows on the veranda as her cheeks must be absolutely scarlet at the moment. "No, they haven't, Captain Bancroft." She hesitated, then plunged on. "That was the first time a gentleman has kissed me."

His brows shot up and his eyes first widened then narrowed. "You've never been kissed? In truth?"

Hanging her head, Emma nodded. "I told you, I've not been out in Society but a little while. I don't know many gentlemen.

And…I wouldn't have wanted to kiss them if I had known them."

"But you wanted to kiss me." His voice sounded so stern.

"Yes," she whispered, wondering how the evening had taken such a horrible turn. Oh, she'd known proper young ladies didn't go about kissing every man they met. She wouldn't do that either. But she'd wanted to kiss Captain Bancroft, whose very presence made her feel safe and secure. She'd no idea it would make him angry. She started for the door. "Perhaps we should go back in the house."

"In a moment." Gently, he lifted her chin until their gazes met. "Why did you want to kiss me?"

His question made her want to squirm like a worm on a hook. She couldn't tell him the truth, that she wanted to kiss him so he'd want to marry her. From what she'd heard, gentlemen didn't like to think themselves trapped into marriage. Not that she wanted to trap Captain Bancroft. But she did want to marry him, now more than ever. "Because I like you."

If that wasn't the whole truth, it was at least partly true.

"I am flattered, Miss Washer." His words were kind but sounded cool. "I like you as well. I simply find it difficult to believe, having kissed you, that I am the first man to do so."

Forgetting to be embarrassed, Emma frowned at him. "I assure you, Captain, you are. I'd expect you to know the difference between a young lady who has never had such attentions before and one who is no better than she should be." Her aunt had spoken of young women of a certain class in Sitapur who she'd described with that moniker. Emma hadn't quite understood at the time, although now she believed she did. "Unless you too had never been kissed until now."

At that, he burst out laughing. "Oh, I assure you, I have had my share of kisses before now. And I would have sworn you had as well." He offered his arm and, grudgingly, she took it. "But I will concede you may simply know how to kiss naturally."

"But I didn't know about…about what you did at the end."

"That's what makes me believe you haven't been kissed

before." He squeezed her arm against his body, sending another streak of heat shooting down to her toes. "Perhaps you might like me to teach you about it some time?"

Emma relaxed against him, holding his arm more tightly. Everything might just work out after all. "Thank you, Captain. I would like that very much…sometime." She smiled into the darkness as they approached the veranda door. "Although, I think at this point, we should dispense with the formalities. Please call me Emma."

"If you will call me Alex."

Her smile broadened as they entered the drawing room. "I am honored, Alex."

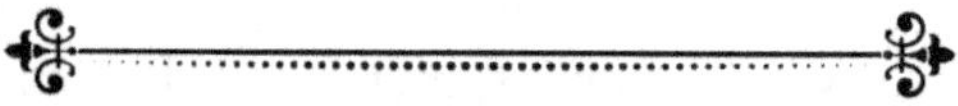

Chapter Four

Running, running this way and that, down this corridor—no, no that was a dead end. She paused for a split second, not knowing which way to go. A huge explosion to her right and she shrieked and ran to her left, down another endless hallway, searching for safety and finding none. Another explosion and rat-tat-tat *of gunfire brought another scream to her lips. Putting her hands over her ears, she darted down the main staircase. Why couldn't she find someone? Someone who would keep her safe in this madness of confusion and noise.*

On the main floor now, she dodged around broken beams and leaped over rubble blocking her way to the outside. To safety. She stumbled and looked down to see the body of her aunt lying lifeless on the floor. No, no, no. She backed away, turned, and ran again, praying for someone to save her. A lone figure stepped out from nowhere—a man dressed in scarlet regimentals. She flew into his arms, burrowed her face into the hard chest, and slumped in relief. Safe at last. Raising her head, she peered up into the handsome face of Captain Alexander Bancroft just as the blast of cannon fire tore them apart.

A crash of thunder brought Emma bolt upright in her bed, heart racing as much from the frightful noise as from the horrible nightmare that had held her in its clutches. Gripping the bedcovers, she peered into the darkness around her, the shadowy shapes striking terror into her already frantic mind. Her eyes finally adjusted to the faint light of the banked fire and she fought to slow her breathing. "I'm safe now, I'm safe now, I'm safe now." Repeating that phrase helped dispel her terror sometimes. Helped her remember she was in England, thousands of miles from anyone who wished her harm. "I'm safe now."

This time, the little catchphrase worked. Moments later, her trembling subsided a little and she released her frantic grip on the covers. This nightmare had been worse than the others, more vivid, more real. Her mind shied away from the memory of it, but the terror lingered. She needed the comfort of light, for a while at least. Hopefully she'd be able to sleep again, eventually.

With shaking hands, she felt for the bedside table, struck a match, and lit the lamp. The pretty little pink and green room she'd been assigned sprang into relief, the fearful shadowy shapes now merely the posters of her bed and the wardrobe in the corner. Emma drew her legs up, wrapped her arms around them, and slowly her heartbeat returned to normal. She always hoped each of these nightmares would be the last, but had come to the sad realization that they likely wouldn't stop anytime soon. Although this one had been somewhat different.

Most of the dream had been the same—the running, the confusion, finding her aunt, rushing down the staircase, discovering the soldier—however, there had been one significant change that had caught her attention even while she was held in the thrall of the dream. Usually, the soldier in regimentals turned out to be Lieutenant (later Captain) Samuel Hill Lawrence, with whom she'd formed an acquaintance that summer of 1857. Tonight, however, she'd been surprised the soldier trying to rescue her had been Captain Bancroft, although perhaps she shouldn't have been. He certainly made her feel every bit as safe as Captain Lawrence had.

"Alex." Simply saying his name aloud sent a frisson of warmth all over her chilled body and some of her fear abated. She lay back and burrowed deeper beneath the covers. She'd been such a wanton woman last evening it was no wonder Alex thought her more experienced than she actually was. She'd not thought of that before she agreed to kiss him.

But that kiss…

The memory of his lips on hers, his big hands cradling her head so gently as he turned it so their mouths fit together perfectly, made her warm all over. Made her tingle in unexpected places. And when he tried to put his tongue into her mouth—

Emma turned over abruptly onto her stomach, burying her head in the pillow. Never had she been so embarrassed in her whole life. She'd told him the truth, though; she'd never been kissed before, never dreamed gentlemen would try to do such things. She supposed once she was married, her husband would wish to do such things as well. Well, if they were married, that should be all right. Alex had said he would teach her more about kissing. If he were her husband, he could teach her so much more…

A longing deep inside her began to spiral upward. She wanted Alex to be her husband, of that she was certain. The safe haven of his arms was like none she'd ever known, and to have that haven forever was her greatest wish. His kisses had left her breathless and tingling, which was certainly a good thing. They'd not known one another very long, but that shouldn't be an impediment if they wished to marry. Society approved of arranged marriages where the parties knew each other not at all. They at least had this house party to get to know one another. If they continued to get along as well as they had so far, Emma had no reason to believe their marriage couldn't take place in short order.

All she had to do now was get him to propose.

EARLY NEXT MORNING, Alex bounded down the stairs, keeping a sharp eye out for Yule. In his hand, he clutched the letter he'd received from their cousin Julius in the first post informing him that he was almost ready to make an offer for Augusta Hardy. That didn't seem right at all, for unless he was very mistaken,

Miss Hardy was in attendance at this very house party. Of course, Jules didn't need to propose to the young lady before speaking to her father, and Alex had no idea if his cousin had been courting Miss Hardy before the wager had been declared. He therefore needed to speak to Yule at once to see if he thought this was actually true or if the missive was merely meant to help goad Alex into marrying the first young lady he could find in order to win the side wager. Alex would put nothing past his cousins in the matter of wagering. He'd noticed Yule speaking animatedly with Lady Cora Hastings last evening when he and Emma had come in from their tete-a-tete on the veranda. His cousins seemed determined to give him a run for his money to see who could marry first.

After last night's kiss on the veranda, however, Alex was convinced his marriage to Miss Washer was all but assured. The young lady seemed more than willing to compromise herself with him. He'd spent a good deal of time last night tossing and turning in his bed wondering if Emma was planning to compromise *him* and thereby assure their nuptials. As far as the wager was concerned, such actions were completely acceptable, although he'd prefer those not be the circumstances to spur the wedding.

Heading toward the breakfast room, Alex kept an eye out for his uncle as well. Even though he'd made some headway toward learning more about Emma and her family, he didn't know nearly enough. Uncle Jack and Aunt Lucinda likely had more information to impart. He'd ferret them out as soon as he consulted with Yule.

As expected, most of the gentlemen were in the breakfast room eating heartily before heading out to the shooting stands, his cousin among them. There was also a fair sprinkling of ladies partaking of the copious number of dishes as well, but Emma wasn't one of them. That suited Alex. He needed to confer with his cousin and uncle before he could claim her company for at least part of the morning. He made his way over to Yule.

Alex slid into a seat next to his cousin just before Lord Taverham could set his plate down. "Pardon me, my lord, but it is imperative that I speak to my cousin this instant."

With a long-suffering sigh, Taverham took himself off to the other end of the table.

"Good morning, cousin."

"Morning." Yule heaped grilled kidneys onto a piece of toast, then cut the bread into four precise squares and began to eat. As he chewed, he gesticulated with his fork, pointing it at the empty space in front of Alex.

"I'll eat later. Right now I need your advice on an important matter." He drew the letter out of his inner pocket. "I received this from Jules this morning. Do you think he's serious?"

Sipping his cup of coffee, that smelled divine, Yule put out his hand. "What's he saying?"

"He's about to ask for Miss Hardy's hand. I'd believe it, except for the fact she's here this weekend and he's not." Alex looked about then waved a footman over. "Coffee with sugar, please, John."

"Very good, Captain Bancroft."

Alex turned back to his cousin, his brow puckered. He'd look a right fool to Grandfather and the others if Julius stole a march on him and married first. "What do you think? Has he been courting her already? Did you know of it?"

"If he's done so, I haven't heard of it." Yule handed the missive back and picked up his fork again. "He may just be having you on." He shrugged and dug into a pungent game pie. "In any case, you seem to be well ahead of the rest of us in the race to matrimony. I noticed you and Miss Washer disappeared onto the veranda last night." He raised his brows at Alex as he prepared to take a bite of pie. "I'm extremely surprised you didn't come back betrothed, or at least compromised."

"We might well have done so had anyone seen us out there." Alex smiled at the memory of Emma's sweet body pressed against him. The softness of her lips, the brush of her breast against his chest. His member stirred strongly, apparently remembering as well. He sat back as the footman set the coffee in front of him, then pulled his chair far forward. No need to advertise his arousal. "But if she continues her flirtation with me, I predict we will be announcing our engagement by the end of the party."

"So much the better for you, I suppose. Do you know if she's well dowered? Or do you care about nothing save winning the wager?" Yule didn't sound put out so much as concerned.

"I'm looking for Uncle Jack as soon as I leave you. I want to check into her circumstances, both financial and social. She's not been very forthcoming about herself and her family."

"Well, at least you're showing some sense and not completely focused on the wager." His cousin raised a brow. "Or are you? Do you really not care if you marry a virtual stranger, Alex? I know it's done by some of Society, but don't you want an inkling that the two of you will suit? That you have a hope of falling in love?"

If Yule had seen them outside last night, he wouldn't have asked that particular question. Grinning, Alex sipped his coffee. "I think Emma and I will have as much of a chance at marital happiness as any other couple. If last night was any indication, we may well have a better one."

"Well, then Godspeed, cousin." Yule tossed his napkin onto the table. "I give you my blessing, even though you don't need it, and my best wishes for your success. As this is Saturday and we all leave Monday, you've got your work cut out for you." He rose. "D'you want to shoot at the same stand? Make a completely different wager for the day? Most birds brought down before luncheon?"

"Tempting, Yule, but I'm not shooting today." Alex sipped more of the excellent coffee. "I want to spend as much time with Miss Washer as I can. Perhaps a game of croquet so I can see how well she shows to advantage at sport."

"My loss then. I'm certain I would have trounced you soundly."

"Not a chance." Alex chuckled, then spied his uncle entering the room in conversation with Lord Braeton. "But don't let me keep you. I need to speak to Uncle Jack before he heads out to the stands. It won't be long now, I think. Good luck."

"Thanks, but I doubt I'll need it." Yule headed out, stopping to speak to Uncle Jack, who immediately turned and headed toward Alex.

"Alex, good morning." His uncle towered over the seat Yule had just vacated. "Mr. Quartermain tells me you wished to speak to me. I'm heading out to the break now. We can speak on the way to the stands."

Rather sheepishly, Alex shook his head. "I hadn't planned to shoot today, uncle."

A look of alarm flashed over his uncle's face. "You're not ill, are you?"

"Oh no, right as rain, my lord."

"Well, thank God for that." The concerned countenance vanished, replaced by a deep frown. "Then what the devil keeps you from shooting with me today?"

Alex shot to his feet. "Let's talk as we walk."

Once they left the breakfast room and were relatively alone, Alex began his plea. "I hate missing the shoot, uncle, but I'd hoped to spend more time with Miss Washer this morning."

"Miss Washer, eh?" Uncle Jack cocked his head. "You spent a goodly amount of time in her company last evening, if I recollect."

"I did, uncle. And we've been getting on so well, I wanted to continue in her company as much as possible this weekend."

"Strike while the iron is hot, hum?"

"Exactly, uncle." Good. He'd be forgiven for abandoning the sport then. "I did wonder if you knew anything about her prospects. I can't ask her, of course, and since she's orphaned, I take it, I don't know to whom I should apply for a formal courtship." Not that he'd have time for such a thing. "She's under the sponsorship of Lady Tilney, I think."

"Yes, that is so, although she wouldn't be the young lady's

guardian. Lord Tilney, perhaps, but he was unable to attend the weekend." Uncle Jack continued down the corridor toward the entry hall. "Both Miss Washer's parents, and now her aunt and uncle who had guardianship of her, have died. I've no idea who that leaves as her closest relatives."

"Her aunt and uncle died?" So great was his surprise, Alex came to a full stop in the middle of the foyer. "She never told me that."

"It happened out in India, although I don't have the particulars." His uncle shook his head as they started outside toward the waiting break.

"Good God, were they killed during the uprising?" His head spinning with this tragic possibility, Alex hurried his pace to keep up.

"Well, Miss Washer just returned this past spring. The mutiny took place—"

"From 1857 until 1859. The primary fighting and bloodshed ended in June of '58, though." Alex had avidly followed the dispatches and newspaper articles on the massacres throughout the conflict, his blood seething with rage at the atrocities. He'd prayed fervently that his regiment would be called to serve there, but to his continued regret, that had not occurred.

"Mr. Washer was a shareholder in the East India Company, so I suppose it's possible." Uncle Jack climbed into the break. "Miss Washer hasn't spoken of it to you?"

"Of this, no, not a word." Could there be another explanation?

"Then take some advice, my boy. Let her tell you of it in her own time." His uncle nodded, a grim look in his eye. "If you try to pry, the fairer sex will withdraw and you never know if they will *ever* speak to you again."

"You sound as though you speak from experience, uncle."

"I do, Alex. Believe me, I do." With a sigh, Uncle Jack sat back in the cart. "We're ready, Norbert," he called to the driver. "Enjoy your morning with Miss Washer, Alex. And if you're in earnest about courting her, let her set the terms." He tapped the side of his nose. "Otherwise, you may be in for a much longer and less pleasant courtship."

"Thank you, uncle. I'll be certain to take your advice." Alex waved as the break moved forward slowly, then turned and strolled back toward the house, hands clasped behind his back. This new information would take some pondering.

If Emma had been caught up in the bloody conflict in India, that would illuminate much about her behavior, especially her affinity for his status as a soldier. Alex longed to go find Emma this instant and ply her with questions; however, his uncle was unerringly correct. Alex must allow Emma to divulge her past to him in her own manner and in her own time.

The problem with that approach lay with their lack of time. The house party would break up on Monday and he had no idea when or where he might meet Emma again. If he was truly contemplating marrying her, and winning his wager, they needed to have the matter settled before the guests departed two days from now.

So he really couldn't let her past be a factor in their courtship. Intriguing as the question might be, it didn't necessarily need to be answered before they married. If it turned out she had survived that horrible uprising, then he could praise her for her endurance and grace under fire. It could prove a fascinating tale for her to relate to him lying comfortably in their bed some night.

Conjuring that image, of him and Emma entwined naked in bed together, had become his favorite way of passing the time when he wasn't physically with her. They would make that vision a reality very soon, of that he was completely sure. No other young lady would do for him now. That had become apparent last evening when he realized Miss Emma Washer was the perfect blend of innocent young lady and wanton siren. That she didn't understand her dual nature gave her a charm he couldn't deny attracted him.

She'd said she wanted him to teach her more about kissing.

Alex grinned as he entered the house. He'd do that with pleasure. And once they married, he could teach her so much more—the many ways a man could please a woman, and how a woman could do the same thing for a man. Thoughts of instructing his wife in the ways of the marriage bed excited him so much—

A savage throb from his member almost stopped him mid-stride. All these thoughts of Emma had aroused him fully, tenting his breeches. It would never do for her to discover him in such a state before their nuptials. Afterwards would be a different story. Now, however, he should make a detour to his room and release his tension alone before seeking her out.

He started up the stairs, taking two at a time. Rounding the newel post on the first floor, he hurried down the corridor toward the gentlemen's wing, praying fervently he met no one, especially not Emma.

CHAPTER FIVE

MONDAY MORNING, DIRECTLY after breakfast, which she could not eat, Emma headed for the rose garden to pace and think.

Alex was leaving this afternoon.

To be sure, all the guests were leaving—herself, Augusta, and Lady Tilney included—but something about the idea that she would have to stand and watch as Alex's carriage sped down the driveway, taking him to the train station and then to London, made her stomach roil as though she might shoot the cat, as the sailors on the *Scotia* said of seasick passengers. She was walking about now to help steady her nerves.

Despite being together with her every day and evening of the house party, Alex still had made no move to propose to her. After he eschewed the shooting on Saturday in favor of playing croquet with her and some of the other young ladies, escorted her to the little country parish church on Sunday morning, and accompanied her, Augusta, and her chaperone to view Winchester Cathedral that afternoon, Emma had been certain he would whisk her off to the veranda last evening, fall to his knee, and propose.

Much to her dismay, he'd stayed overly long in the smoking room after dinner, he and his uncle being the last ones to enter the drawing room. When he'd finally approached her, he'd been cordial, but had kept their conversation to the most general of topics, mostly about the wretched cathedral they'd just visited. Had he lost interest so quickly? Had he decided she was too wanton after all? They hadn't kissed again; they'd had no opportunity to do so last evening or the one before. She'd hoped she would have at least had one more chance to kiss him before they parted ways. The thought that she would not be able to do so saddened her very much indeed.

She supposed she could discover if Alex would be attending entertainments in London in the autumn and ask Lady Tilney if they could travel to Town for the Little Season. Somehow, she doubted he'd have leave from his regiment to do so, but she could inquire. The lovely morning seemed robbed of its glory, as though out of nowhere, dark gray thunderclouds had suddenly covered the clear blue sky.

How had she come to long for Captain Alexander Bancroft's company in so short a time? She'd met other men in uniform, and although she'd enjoyed the safety their bright garb had instilled in her, something else about Alex—she couldn't quite put her finger on it—touched a chord deep within her. Safety, of course, but a strange stirring as well whenever she called his face to mind. She'd been so certain he was searching for a wife she'd almost taken it for granted that he'd propose.

Emma pulled her white silk lace shawl around her shoulders. One really should not count their chickens, as her aunt used to admonish her. Raising her chin, Emma continued toward the back of the rose garden to the beautiful bower at the far end. If he didn't propose, if she couldn't bring him up to scratch during the Little Season, then she'd have to move on, try to find another man who made her feel as safe as Alex did. A tall order, of course, and barring that she'd have to accept some other gentleman. She'd imposed on Lord and Lady Tilney's kindness quite enough. At the end of June, she'd turned one and twenty, so she now could make some of her own decisions at least. More than anything, she wanted a home of her own. But to obtain that, she needed a husband.

"Emma."

She whirled around to find herself face to face with Alex. Apparently, he had more stealth than any cat she'd ever known. Her cheeks heated until they must look like two ripe apples. That could be accounted for by the heat, perhaps. "Alex, good morning. I wasn't certain I'd see you before we left."

"Did you think I'd let you escape off to London or some remote county seat without saying a single goodbye?" His admonition sounded teasing, but there was a serious glint in his eyes.

"I should certainly hope not, sir." Smiling, she took his arm, once more thrilling at the strength of it, at the immediate sense of calm that came over her whenever she touched him. "But we didn't get to speak much last evening and you might have had an early train."

"On the contrary, I hope to spend a few more days here with my aunt and uncle." His serious tone disappeared altogether. "Do you think we might prevail upon Lady Tilney to stay a few more days as well?"

Emma's heart took off racing like a thoroughbred on Derby Day. "Oh, I do hope so." She glanced around the rose garden, happier now than she had been in so very long. "Caxton Park has such a pleasant prospect. I know I would enjoy seeing the many walks and sights around the estate and village." She squeezed his arm. "Especially with you as my guide."

"That does sound delightful, doesn't it?" They strolled along the crushed shell path, the warm breeze wafting the glorious scent of roses all about them. "Have you walked as far as the bower before?" He gestured to the structure at the end of the path, a framework of metal to which several different roses—pink, white, and yellow—clung so thickly as to create a little room. Inside stood a wooden swing wide enough for two. "It's the prettiest spot in the garden, in my opinion."

"I did see it on my first day here. I love gardens, so walked all over this one." Emma wanted to be truthful, but she didn't want to pass up any opportunity with Alex. "I didn't actually get to swing in it, though. I was with Augusta and she did not wish to linger." Smiling up at him, she prayed with all her might that if they sat on the swing together, he would kiss her again. "I would like to give it a try this time, if I may."

"As you wish, my dear."

The look in his eyes was so warm Emma thought she would melt on the spot. Why must she wear so many layers in the heat? She allowed her shawl to slip from her shoulders until it was hanging down her back. It made no difference in any case. As long as she was in Alex's company, she'd be as hot as if she stood in a furnace.

As soon as they reached the flowered arbor, Emma ducked into its shadowy depths. Its coolness came as a welcomed surprise and the perfume of the overhanging blooms made her head spin with the heavy scent. Alex held the swing and she sank onto it gratefully. Between the heat without, the sudden coolness within, the intense sweetness of the flowers, and Alex's presence, her head had begun to spin. She glanced up at him and patted the seat by her. "Will you sit beside me?"

"In a moment, perhaps." He strode to the edge of the bower and peered down the path they'd just taken. His head moved back and forth as he scanned the garden, then apparently satisfied with what he saw, Alex turned back to her. "Good. It seems we are very much alone."

Emma's eyes widened and her breath caught in her throat as he dropped gracefully to one knee and took her hand.

"We have known one another for only a matter of days, Emma, but I believe you to be the loveliest woman of my acquaintance. Sweet, kind, beautiful..." He grinned. "And the tiniest bit naughty, making you the perfect woman for me."

Gazing into his deep blue eyes staring so intently at her, Emma could scarcely breathe beyond little hitching gasps. Was this real? Was she about to hear the question she'd longed to answer ever since seeing him...was it only three days ago? Her hands trembled in his grip. Dear God, don't let her faint.

"Miss Washer...Emma, will you do me the greatest honor in the world and consent to be my wife?"

Seized by an emotion so great it stripped her of the power of speech, Emma could only grip his hand tightly and nod enthusiastically.

Alex waited, cocking his head as he gazed at her. "Is that a yes, sweetheart?"

"Yes!" It came out as an explosive gasp, but at last it was out. "Yes, yes, yes, Alex, I will marry you." She wanted to get up and shout, twirl around beneath the arbor. Safe at last. With total abandon, she threw her arms around him and whispered in his ear, "Thank you."

"My pleasure, darling." He rose, bringing her to her feet as well. "Now that we're allowed to kiss any time we want, would you like that lesson I promised you Friday night?"

"Yes." Her voice was husky from a newfound, deep-seated desire to feel his lips on hers once more. She slid her arms up around his neck. "Yes, please, Alex."

With a wolfish grin, he lowered his mouth to hers and the world melted away. Insistent lips pressed hers and she pushed back, not knowing what she was doing, but willing to try anything at this point. His strong arms squeezed her to his hard chest until her breasts were all but flattened against him. The ache in them grew, feeding the throbbing sensation between her legs. That hadn't happened the last time they kissed. Was this one of the lessons she needed to learn?

Her attention sprang back to her lips as Alex slid his tongue along the seam, pressing gently, seeking entry. Very well. They were about to be married. It was time she learned more about how a gentleman kissed his wife. Hesitantly, Emma relaxed her mouth a little, then more, then... Her lips parted swiftly as Alex's tongue slid into her mouth.

The sensation was so foreign she couldn't tell if she liked it or not. At least she'd been expecting it this time and didn't balk as she had before. Concentrating on Alex's movements, Emma stood perfectly still, eyes closed, seeing what he was doing with her mind's eye. He plundered here and there, now tickling the roof of her mouth—which elicited a squeal from her—now thrusting in and out with a fiercely pounding beat that enflamed the throbbing at her core. She groaned, maddened that she didn't know what to do other than simply stand there and let him have his way with her. He certainly didn't seem to mind.

In fact, he'd begun to groan as well, each thrust of his tongue lingering inside a little longer. With so many new sensations bombarding everywhere on her body, Emma's legs began to grow weak. She hitched herself closer to Alex, trying to find a way to rest against him. Suddenly, his hand cupped her buttocks, and before she could protest, he lifted her up and laid her back on the swing, not breaking the kiss all the while. Head whirling, Emma could do nothing save lay back panting, enjoying everything he was doing though she understood none of it.

With a swift movement, Alex sprawled himself on the swing beside her, breaking the kiss at last. "First lesson is complete." He raised a brow. "Did you enjoy it?"

Scarcely able to speak, Emma nodded and finally squeaked out, "Very much."

"Time for lesson two?"

Dazed, she nodded, unable to imagine what he might do next.

"Good." He leaned over, his mouth beside her ear sending warmth cascading down her spine. "I'm going to touch you."

What did he mean? "But you've been touching me."

"Skin to skin." Alex slid his hand down her décolletage and wormed his way beneath her corset until his finger rested at the very tip of her breast. "Like that."

Fire leaped into her face. No one had ever touched her *like that*. It was scandalous, it was depraved, it was...wonderful. Alex fondled her nipple, circling it, flicking the tip until each stroke sent a wave of pleasure throughout her body. "Do you like that?"

"Yes. Oh, yes." She pulled him closer, amazed at everything happening to her.

"So sweet." He burrowed his face into her neck, withdrew his hand, then reached down and worked it underneath her skirts.

"Oh, oh, Alex." His hand met the silk stocking that covered her ankle, slid up her calf, beneath her pantalettes to her bare knee, then her hip. Each place he touched stoked a fire deep within her. Good lord, was he heading for her most intimate place? Was that where the mystery of the marriage bed ended? Her heart sped up, beating like a drum in her chest.

"Trust me, sweetheart." He nuzzled her neck again, and Emma was so caught up in his caresses she couldn't say no had she wanted to. His hand slid up further to her—

Crack!

The rope holding up the end of the swing Alex sat on broke, sliding him onto the ground and tumbling Emma down on top of him.

"Oof!" Alex's breath went out with a whoosh.

"Oh, dear. I'm so sorry." Emma scrambled to her feet, blinking at the sun as she crawled out from the bower, panting as her heart began to slow. The spell she'd been under had been broken, thank goodness. Not that she regretted any of her lessons. "Are you all right?"

"Fine." Alex got up slowly, his face flushed.

"Perhaps we should go back to the manor now. We must tell Lady Tilney and Augusta, and your aunt and uncle. And be sure to arrange for our extended stay." Emma couldn't help but smile. All her dreams had come true this morning—who knew what might be in store this afternoon? "Shall we?"

Slowly, Alex offered his arm, then winced when she took it enthusiastically.

"Is something wrong, my dear?" She hoped he hadn't been hurt when the swing broke.

Alex shook his head and started stiffly down the pathway. "Nothing a cold bath won't cure, my love."

Chapter Six

"Repeat after me. I, Emma Elizabeth Washer, take thee, Alexander Percy Bancroft, to be my wedded husband." Reverend Carstairs's sonorous voice filled the small village church near Caxton Park, making Alex wince not for the first time during his marriage ceremony. The vicar's voice was so loud it could rival the last trump and raise the dead.

Amazed that he had gotten his way about virtually everything to do with the wedding, Alex couldn't take his gaze from his beautiful bride's radiant face. Impossible to believe that he'd met her only one week ago today, and yet she'd agreed to marry him. He'd been ready for her to refuse to marry so quickly—and had been astonished when she'd agreed to forego the usual six-month engagement in favor of wedding him on Friday. In order to do so, she'd also eschewed the lavish wedding Lady Tilney had proposed and now stood up in her best day gown of frilly white muslin with accents of red, her sole bridesmaid her friend Augusta. Yet she was still a radiant bride.

"For better or worse, for richer or poorer, in sickness and in health, to love, cherish, and obey, 'til death do us part." Emma looked boldly into his eyes as she spoke her vows, melting his heart a little and arousing him quite a lot. They had been together almost constantly ever since he proposed, yet after that fiery interlude in the bower swing, they'd scarcely had a moment alone. That unfortunate period of celibacy would end this evening, thank God. Now he was merely counting the minutes until the wedding night.

For days he'd pondered why his attraction to her was mostly sexual. They didn't know one another very well still, but he liked her quite a lot. She was an intelligent young woman and had revealed frank opinions about several topics that had surprised him. Vivacious when they talked, she possessed a secretive air when they fell silent. She was beautiful without question, and a genuinely kind person from everything he'd seen. Yet with all these sterling attributes, his primary thoughts at this most solemn moment were not about beginning a life together with Emma, but about them being tangled up in bedsheets. Would he ever come to have the affection for her other men had for their wives? And most importantly, was he doing her a grave disservice by using her to win his wager without telling her?

"I pronounce that they be man and wife together," the reverend intoned, bringing Alex's attention back where it should have been all along. "In the Name of the Father, and of the Son, and of the Holy Ghost. Amen."

As Reverend Carstairs droned on, Alex continued to gaze into Emma's eyes and she into his, her smile widening with each word that bound them irrevocably together. Such shining trust in him would not be misplaced. He would make it his most sacred duty to take care of Emma, to cherish her, and to never make her regret she'd married him.

"This way, Captain." Carstairs motioned them toward a door on the right. Alex offered his arm to Emma and they entered the vestry to sign the registry. Emma went first, her hand steady as she signed her full maiden name for the very last time. His hand, however, shook more than a little as he scratched out his signature.

Then they were back in the chancel, turned toward the congregation of guests, almost all his relations. Grinning ear to ear, Uncle Jack, his best man, gave him a little push to start them down the aisle. Eyes forward, they'd been strictly instructed. Look neither right nor left. For some unknown reason, it was considered in bad taste to acknowledge the presence of the guests. Never mind that. All he wanted to do was look at Emma, his bride. They arrived at the entry hall and he turned toward her. "May I kiss the bride, Mrs. Bancroft?"

"Yes, you may, Captain Bancroft." She grasped him around the neck and pulled him down to her. "I was hoping you would ask."

"HERE'S TO THE happy couple and to a wager well won." Grandfather raised a glass of champagne and all of Alex's cousins did the same, toasting him in a private corner of the drawing room. Such a gratifying moment. Alex raised his glass as well, savoring his victory.

The wedding breakfast, given by Aunt Lucinda, had turned out well, despite the rush to complete all the details in just three days. He and Emma had returned from the church and been placed in a corner of the drawing room surrounded by such huge bunches of flowers Alex wondered if the gardener had stripped every bloom from the garden. They'd greeted everyone in the receiving line, and he'd had the pleasure of introducing Emma to all his family. Once the line had ended, her bridesmaid and Aunt Lucinda had whisked her away for what purpose Alex didn't know. He'd gravitated toward his male kinfolk, all of whom congratulated him soundly on winning the wager.

That was why he was keeping a lookout for his bride, determined to prevent her from knowing about the marriage wager, at least until her wedding day had ended. Not until he was standing in the receiving line, Emma smiling so happily beside him, did it occur to him she might be upset to know he'd married her on a bet. He hated to think she might be hurt to find out he'd had ulterior motives for their marriage, although he'd assure her they weren't the only ones. When he looked at his beautiful bride, he swelled with pride. Somehow, he'd have to convince her he'd have married her even without the wager.

"Now that the first of you is married, who do you think will be the next one to get tie the knot?" Grinning like a lunatic, Grandfather gazed from one cousin to the next. "Yule? Want to take that up?"

Yule shook his head. "No, Grandfather. Alex may have found a wife out of hand, but I think I'll take my time. I may be the last of us to take the plunge."

"Huh." The old man wheeled around and glared at Francis. "What about you, sir? Will you take the wager?"

"Not for every gold guinea in the Bank of England." His cousin crossed his arms, calmly standing his ground.

"And why not, sir? You agreed to the larger wager. Why not get the matter done like Alex?" He had to give it to Grandfather. The man knew what he wanted. "I'll sweeten the wager handsomely if you do, Hamerton."

Francis looked as though he was caught between Scylla and Charybdis and seasick to boot. "How sweet, Grandfather?"

"There we go. There's the Quartermain in you. Never turn down a wager." He held out his glass. "Footman, pour."

The nearest servant scurried forward, pouring champagne into the glass until it neared the rim. Grandfather sipped, nodded, and the footman darted away. "I'll wager 500 guineas on the matter. Who'll take it?"

"I'm not wagering on this, Grandfather." A sharpness in Francis's tone quelled the rising voices. "You have my word on it. I…It may take me some time to bring the lady I've chosen around to the idea of marrying me."

"Oh, but that is wonderful. Side bet!" Tom piped up and came forward to jostle Francis's elbow. "I say Francis can't bring her up to snuff until after Christmas."

If looks were arrows, Tom would have been dead on the

spot. Francis glared at him. "No bets on me, if you please. I cannot have the wager come to the lady's ears. All hope would be lost."

"What hope is lost?"

Alex spun around, his stomach brushing his boots. He'd been so engrossed in the wagering he'd forgotten to look out for Emma. "Hello, my dear." He kissed her temple and snuck his arm around her waist. "What have you been up to?"

"Aunt Lucinda," Emma blushed and dropped her head. "She asked me to call her that. I hope you don't mind."

"Not at all. What did she do with you?"

"She and Augusta took me out to the garden and made me tell them how the bower swing broke."

Alex choked, coughed, and finally caught his breath. Thank goodness he and Emma were now married, but neither lady should have heard about that scandalous rendezvous. "What did you tell them, my love?"

"Only what happened, my dear. I was sitting on the swing, and you proposed, and I was so overcome I swooned back on the swing." She put the back of her hand to her forehead and leaned back against Alex's arm. "You sat down on it to try and fan me, and our combined weight proved too much for the old rope."

"And was that the truth, Mrs. Bancroft?" Sandy had been watching Emma keenly as she told her tale.

Grinning at his cousin, Emma smoothed out her gown with several light touches. "As much of the truth as they needed to know, my lord."

"I see you chose wisely, Alex." Sandy bowed to Emma. "I'd wager you have a perfect poker face, Mrs. Bancroft, wouldn't you, Tom? As the newest member of the family, we'd all love to include you in our family wagers."

Alex stiffened. This was getting all too close to disclosing the marriage wager for his comfort. He had to change the subject or simply take Emma away before his relatives made his life miserable—on his wedding day, no less. "Didn't Aunt Lucinda say we needed to cut the cakes just before we leave, sweetheart?" He pulled out his pocket watch, hoping against hope it was close to time for them to go. "Almost time, my dear." He grasped her hand and pulled it through his arm. "Mustn't keep everyone waiting."

"Nonsense, Alex. It's just after half-past one." The fiendish Tom spoke up brightly. "You've got plenty of time. Allow your bride to partake in her first wager as a Quartermain."

Alex held his breath. Tom could be wild, but he wouldn't knowingly do something to hurt a lady. Clenching his fist, Alex's stare bored into Tom's amused face. He shook his head once. A shot across the bow. "I think it's time for us to go now."

Tom raised a brow, then shook his head as well. "I'm sorry, I misspoke, Mrs. Bancroft. I'd forgotten you've already been part of one of our wagers, hasn't she, Alex?"

As though a red veil had descended over his eyes, Alex couldn't see anything save Tom's grinning face. Didn't want to see anything but his fist putting his cousin's lights out.

"What does he mean, Alex?" Emma had turned to him, her brows in a deep V. "What wager have I been party to?"

"Our family wager, young lady." To Alex's horror, his grandfather strode forward. "I began it not long ago, wagering my six grandsons of marriageable age couldn't all get married within one year. If they do, I will give them lands and money enough to set them up well to begin their married lives. If even one of them does not marry within the prescribed time, none of them will see a single penny." To Alex's astonishment, Grandfather took Emma's arm and patted her hand. "So you see, my dear, you have done your duty and set an example for the rest of these rascals as to why they should find good wives."

The smile on Emma's face seemed plastered there, for Grandfather's benefit most likely. Alex swallowed convulsively. His wedding day was now a shambles and they had yet to even board the train to London.

"Your Grace." Emma's voice was steady, respectful. Her gaze

at Alex, however, seethed with anger. "Was there a stipulation that the prospective brides could not know about the wager?"

Every gaze turned toward Grandfather. Would the man tell a lie to save his grandson's marriage?

"No, my dear." He shook his head gently and Alex's hopes sank. "There was no such stipulation." He shot a stern look at Alex. "You mean he didn't tell you about the wager?"

"He did not." Emma rounded on Alex, her face pinched, and he braced himself to have a public drubbing such as he'd never had before. "I only wish he had."

Alex's jaw dropped open and remained that way for quite some moments. Finally, he pulled himself together. "Wh...what do you mean, my dear?"

"I mean I wouldn't have fretted so much about whether or not you were planning to propose to me had I known there was a wager working on my behalf." The stern façade melted bit by bit until his wife stood before him, smiling and somehow triumphant. "Take my advice, gentlemen, and let your ladies know what's afoot. Honesty will always stand you in good stead."

As stunned as Alex, his cousins merely nodded while his grandfather chuckled and sipped his champagne.

"And now, my dear, I believe we are called to cut the cakes." She took Alex's arm and nodded to his family. "Be sure you come to get your slices, gentlemen. Mrs. Pierce and the kitchen maids have been working day and night to produce these lovely cakes for our wedding. You mustn't miss them." She leaned toward the nearest cousin, who happened to be Sandy. "I wager they'll prove good luck for your endeavors." With a twitch of her hooped skirts, Emma led them away from his stunned cousins.

Before they moved out of earshot, Grandfather tugged on Alex's arm and he stopped.

"Congratulations, my boy. You chose very wisely."

CHAPTER SEVEN

"AND YOU'RE CERTAIN you didn't mind?"

Alex had asked Emma that same question at least twenty times since they'd boarded the train in Hampshire. Now they were in the hack, heading for their newly rented home, and he apparently still wasn't convinced. Her answer had been the same each time, but she was getting weary replying. "Alex, how many times do I have to tell you no, I don't mind that you wagered you would marry within the year nor that you further wagered you would be the first to marry. I wouldn't even have cared if you had wagered you would marry me in particular." She cocked her head at him. "That wasn't part of the wager, was it?"

Shaking his head, Alex mumbled, "No."

"And it wouldn't have mattered if it had been." She grasped his chin and guided his face until he looked straight at her. "I told you before, I set my cap for you the moment I saw you from up on the staircase."

"But why?" He peered at her, his brow furrowed like rows of corn turned by a plow. "Why would you do such a thing?"

While it was on the tip of her tongue to say, "It was your regimentals," she thought better of that, but told the truth nevertheless. "What young lady with a grain of sense wouldn't find a handsome young man, so dashing in his uniform, attractive?" She ran her hand through his hair. "Especially one with such dark, curly hair."

He grabbed her hand and kissed it, sending a wave of warmth up her arm. "You won't regret marrying me, Emma. I swear it."

Gazing into his earnest face, her heart ached. Theirs might not be a love match, as other young ladies she knew of boasted, but they would be happy together. Of that she'd make certain. "No, Alex." She squeezed his hand. "I never will, my dear."

They rode on in companionable silence for another few blocks until the carriage pulled up in front of a tall red-brick townhouse, white marble steps leading up to the carved oak door with brass knocker. Emma craned her head back, staring up at the three-storied building. "Are we living here?"

"Thanks to Uncle Jack. He insisted on taking it for us until my regiment gets its next assignment." Alex bounded down from the carriage and offered her his hand. "We should remain in London for the next three months at least, so I've been told. After that, Mrs. Bancroft," he grabbed her up in his arms before she could take a step, "you will be following the drum to wherever I go."

"Ahhgh! Alex, what are you doing?"

He whirled her around on the pavement before running up the steps and pounding on the door. "Carrying you across the threshold, as any proper groom would do to his bride."

Well, that was quite romantic. Perhaps things were looking up.

The door opened on a servant whose brows flew upward. "Captain Bancroft?"

"Yes…uh, you're the butler?" Alex smiled and shifted his weight back and forth as though eager to move forward.

"Yes, Buckleigh, sir."

"Good. Buckleigh, see to the bags, please. The rest of Mrs. Bancroft's things will arrive in a day or two."

"Very good, sir." The butler stepped aside nimbly as Alex pushed past him into the foyer so abruptly Emma had to throw her arms around his neck to keep herself from falling.

"I see someone is eager to see our new home." She was so

close to his face she could see the flash of fire in his eyes.

"You are correct." He slid her down the front of him, every inch of them touching until her feet landed on the black tile floor of the foyer. "Would you like to explore it with me?"

"Yes." Her voice breathy from the intimate contact, Emma nodded as well. The afternoon sun streamed through the windows in the parlor to the right. Long hours before the darkness of the night would signal it was time for them to engage in even more intimacies. Sighing, she took his hand. At least they could endure the wait together. She stuck her head into the room. "I suppose this is the parlor."

The walls were painted a bright sandy beige and half the room sported bookcases filled with books. The windows were decorated with delightful medallions of stained glass that looked like a medieval shield of blue and yellow. A masculine touch, but she liked it. It was furnished with a brown leather sofa and chair, a Queen Anne chair in blue near a matching lady's writing desk in the corner, and a blue-and-green flowered chaise before the fireplace. The wooden floors might benefit from a good quality carpet, perhaps a blue and cream Aubusson.

"Or a library." Alex pulled her over to one of the bookcases and ran a hand over the bindings. "This could easily be turned into a gentleman's room."

"That depends."

"On what?"

"On what would then become the lady's room."

He grinned at her and pulled her in for a kiss. "Fair enough, my lady." Insistent lips on hers took her breath away. "Let us see what the rear of the house holds." He took her hand and Emma was hard pressed to keep up. She'd felt that kiss down to her toes and her knees were still weak.

Their shoes tapped quickly on the hardwood planks as they made their way to the back of the first floor. There, two drawing rooms sat side-by-side, both painted a rich burgundy and divided by a set of folding doors that could turn the two chambers into one large one. The furnishings here were sofas and chairs and curtains in fashionable darker colors of deep green, maroon, and blue.

"Quite an opportunity for entertaining, wouldn't you say, my love?" Alex pulled her into position for a waltz. "Ta da da da da, dum, dum dum da dum, ta da da da da…" He hummed loudly and began to twirl her around the room.

Laughing from sheer joy, Emma eagerly followed his lead, gazing into his eyes, not thinking about the steps at all but simply allowing him to take her wherever he wished. The relief of being in his strong, capable arms made her giddy. She was safe now. No one would ever frighten or hurt her again.

Slowly, they halted until they stood swaying together, lost in each other's embrace.

"Captain Bancroft?"

Emma gasped and jumped away. They couldn't be caught this way… Oh, wait. Yes, they could.

Alex blinked and turned toward the door.

An imposing older woman dressed in black entered the chamber. "There you are, Captain Bancroft. I am Mrs. Dowland, your housekeeper for the duration."

"How do you do, Mrs. Dowland?" Alex gave a short nod and took Emma's hand. "My wife, Mrs. Bancroft."

"Good afternoon, ma'am." Mrs. Dowland dipped a curtsey. "I do apologize, sir, ma'am, that I was not at the door to greet you upon your arrival. I was at the rear door supervising a delivery, but I came as soon as Mr. Buckleigh informed me you had arrived."

"That is perfectly all right, Mrs. Dowland. The situation is new for us all." He smiled down at Emma. "We were just married this morning."

"May I wish you happy, as they said in the old days, Mrs. Bancroft?" The housekeeper smiled warmly at Emma, who sighed with relief. She'd never worked with the upper servants before and the prospect frightened her a little. But she must push forward and learn so she could run Alex's home efficiently.

"Thank you, Mrs. Dowland. We hope to be very happy both here and in our marriage." Clinging to her husband's arm, she prayed she spoke the truth.

"If you will allow me, Captain, ma'am, I can show you the rest of the house before you dress for dinner." With a nod, the housekeeper swept out of the room, leading them down the corridor to the narrow main staircase. "As you've seen the first floor, all that's left is the second floor bedrooms, bathroom, and lady's sitting room. The third floor has three smaller bedrooms, and the attic, where the servants are housed."

"What other servants have been engaged, Mrs. Dowland?" A very important question given she'd no idea how many it would take to run her establishment.

"A housemaid, a scullery maid, a footman, and a cook, ma'am. I think we can manage with that. If not, I'll let you know." Mrs. Dowland turned to Emma. "When will your lady's maid arrive, Mrs. Bancroft?"

Emma sent a panicked look to Alex. Until this morning, she'd been attended by Marks, Augusta's lady's maid. "I fear I shall have to advertise, Mrs. Dowland. We married so quickly I've not had time to engage a maid of my own. Until I'm able to, might the housemaid step into that position?"

"I will perform that service for you, Mrs. Bancroft." The housekeeper looked at her and shook her head. "Angela is as good a housemaid as they come, but she's rather shy and I doubt will be suitable for that task for even a short time. I will be happy to assist you until you can hire someone."

"Thank you, Mrs. Dowland." The offer was very generous and Emma was more than willing to accept it. There was so much to do now that she was the mistress of her own establishment. Her aunt and uncle had traveled so much they had never had a home where they stayed for any length of time. Emma had grown up used to having servants who belonged to someone else.

"Here is the second floor. This room, across from the master bedroom, seems to be the lady's morning room. You may wish to write your letters and have your friends attend you here." She opened the door on a sunny room, painted pale yellow with a theme of ivy and roses in the chaise, chairs, and drapes.

Such a pretty, feminine room made Emma beam broadly. "Oh, yes. I can see myself spending much of my time here."

Alex, who had fallen oddly silent, merely nodded. "I'm certain you will enjoy it, my dear." He turned to the housekeeper. "Mrs. Dowland, might we save the rest of the tour for another time? My wife and I are rather fatigued and wish to retire until dinner."

"Of course, Captain. The master bedroom is just here." She opened the door behind them onto a large bedchamber, the main component being a massive four-poster oak bed jutting majestically into the center of the room. The covers and bedcurtains were again in masculine colors of maroon and blue, and the walls papered in a dark floral paisley that Emma loved on sight. "I see Buckleigh and James have put your things there." She motioned to their trunks. "I'll make sure you are undisturbed until the dinner gong sounds. Do you prefer to dine at seven or eight o'clock?"

"Eight," Alex replied quickly. "Thank you, Mrs. Dowland. You've been a great help. That will be all for now."

"Very good, Captain." With one last nod and a hint of a smile, Mrs. Dowland left, pulling the door closed.

"At last. I thought she'd never leave." Alex turned to Emma, pulled her close, and sank his mouth down on hers.

When they finally came up for air, Emma's head was whirling. "I thought you said we needed to rest."

"I said we needed to retire." He'd already begun pulling at his cravat, his gaze darkening when it fell on her. "Are you tired, my love?" Unbuttoning his jacket in record speed, Alex stripped it from his body and tossed it over his shoulder. "Do you need rest...or something else, perhaps?"

"B...but it's still daylight." She'd always assumed for some reason that marital relations were relegated to the hours of darkness, perhaps because they were too intimate to be done in the light of day. Maybe she'd been wrong about that.

"All the better to see your beauty, my dear." He pulled his shirt out of his breeches, his hair now in wild array. Capturing her chin in his hand, he feathered another kiss over her lips, sending chills down her spine. "Shall I help you disrobe?"

"Yes, please." What else could she say? They were married after all. This was the natural order of things, although she still didn't think it correct to do it in the daytime. Still, her body went from hot to cold by turns just from the way Alex looked at her. Once he began to touch her in earnest…

Her two-piece blue traveling gown buttoned down the front and Alex began on those, his large fingers uncannily nimble as he undressed her. The jacket came away, revealing her sheer white blouse and the corset beneath.

Alex sucked in air then emitted a groan. "Are you very attached to this blouse?"

"This blouse?" Emma looked up at him, uncomprehending. "Not really, n—"

Before she could get the word out, her husband grasped the fabric in both hands and tore the garment in two.

"Alex!"

He buried his face in the deep decolletage of her corset and Emma gasped as his tongue stroked the V in between her breasts. "Oh, Emma, you are so beautiful."

Heat washed over her, her cheeks blazing like two furnaces. Inside, at her core, another fire sprang to life, like the one that had occurred on the swing with Alex. That had also transpired during the day, now that she thought of it. Perhaps the daytime was the right time for them to be together. Pushing her breasts together, Emma deepened the valley between them and thrust them toward her husband.

His groan became an outright moan as he kneaded her breasts together, pulling and kissing them as Emma's core picked up the rhythm. She wrapped her arms around his head, unwilling to have him stop or move away. He worked some more with his hands, and suddenly, cool air touched her where it had been warm just a moment before. Glancing down, she was shocked to see her bare flesh exposed to her husband's avid and approving gaze.

"Emma, my God, you're magnificent."

Her nipples had peaked, furled into tight little points, incredibly sensitive to the touch. And he was touching her. Running his hands over both her breasts, drawing his fingers downward until they cupped the hard tips. She shrugged and the corset slid off, leaving her half naked to his gaze.

All the wantonness from earlier in the week surfaced, making Emma bold. She reached around behind her and untied the tapes that kept her skirt, petticoat, and hoops secured. They fell to the floor with a plop, leaving Emma standing in her pantalettes, stockings, and shoes. A tug on the strings at the back of the drawers and they had pooled at her feet.

Her husband's ragged breathing brought her up short. He stared at her, his gaze starting at her breasts, then traveling over her stomach to her hips, and finally coming to rest on the nest of dark curls at the apex of her thighs. He licked his lips, then his gaze sought her face once more. "Emma, I…I don't know what to say. You are simply the most beautiful woman I have ever seen."

The admiration in his eyes was real, of that she had no doubt. But he needed to move past that because her skin was beginning to pucker with the cold. And anticipation. She rubbed her hands up and down her arms, trying to encourage herself. "I'm sorry, Alex. It's a little chilly now."

"Are you cold, love? Here, let me warm you." He scooped her up and deposited her on the covers. After the initial shock of the cold covers, her back and buttocks began to warm a bit. She stared, fascinated as her husband finished stripping himself so quickly he seemed to have four hands. Boots toppled to the floor, followed by stockings, and then his trousers, shucked off in record time. That left him wearing only his shirt, the tails of which could ill disguise his eager arousal.

Trembling, Emma lay on the cover, pushing herself backward until her head reached the pillows. She quickly pulled off her stockings—her shoes had fallen off when Alex scooped her up in his arms, then crawled under the sheets, not minding the cold at all now, just enthralled by the almost naked form of her husband stalking toward the bed with determined strides. Emma threw the coverlet back and patted the mattress beside her. "Come to bed, my dear."

In one smooth movement, Alex pulled his shirt over his head, leaving him as naked to her gaze as she was to his. She had a fleeting glimpse of a broad chest, barren of hair, wide shoulders, and a waist that tapered to slim hips—where his massive member jutted out.

Alex slipped into bed and pulled the covers over him before Emma could get a good look at him. She wasn't certain that was a good thing. Imagination could make anything better or worse. Her trembling increased.

He pulled her to his extremely warm chest, cradling her against him. "Is that better?"

She nodded, too overcome with the moment to speak.

"Did Lady Tilney tell you what will happen next?" His voice was gentle, but there was an urgency beneath it that couldn't be denied.

Wouldn't be denied, she suspected, even had she wanted to. Which she didn't. Despite her trepidations, she wanted the full experience of marriage to Alex, even knowing what that entailed. "Not Lady Tilney, but yes, I know."

"So you know it will hurt the first time?" He'd pulled her close enough that his breath was hot in her ear.

"Yes." She'd been told that didn't last long, though. "I'm ready."

"As am I, sweetheart. So ready for you." He pressed her back into the mattress, his mouth starting at her ear, then sliding down her throat to her breast. Every inch of her he touched smoldered, every stroke of his tongue produced a glowing red-hot ember until, when his lips closed around her nipple, she burst into flame all over.

"Oh, Alex." His name came out a deep guttural groan even as her core ached for more. There was more, she knew it. How did she ask him—

He lay his hand on her bare knee and she flinched, caught off guard.

"Easy, sweet. Let me do something I think you'll like."

She nodded, completely aware of his fingers stroking her thigh upward, moving toward the place no one had ever—

Gracious! She jumped and gasped as his fingers brushed the thatch of curls at the top of her thighs. Even if she expected something of the sort, to have his hand there, his fingers swirling around that most intimate part of her seemed odd. Felt…good.

He pressed firmly and Emma moaned deep in her throat. What was he doing that made her feel as though she was spiraling upward, toward she knew not what but wanted so badly? Without knowing why, she twitched her hips, pressing toward his hand. One of his fingers touched something, she had no idea what, but—

"Alex! Alex!" Her back arched, her hips bucked, her core exploded with a throbbing ache that gave her so much pleasure she sobbed with the wonder of it all. Clutching his arms, Emma's ragged breathing couldn't calm because Alex kept stroking her, pulling every ounce of pleasure out of her. Panting as though she'd run a race, she gazed into his face. "What…what happened?'

He released a sigh and smiled tenderly down at her. "You just had your first taste of pleasure, love. Did you like it?"

"Oh, yes. I did." She frowned. Indeed, there had been so much pleasure. But… "There wasn't any pain."

"No, there wasn't, sweetheart. What I did just now wasn't

the ultimate intimacy between a man and a woman." Alex shifted his weight until he held himself directly over the top of her. "I wanted you to have the pleasure first. That helps make you ready for me." He pushed his knee between her legs. "Open wider for me, darling."

Weary, and nervous again, Emma did as he asked.

"Try to relax, sweet." He kissed her again, thrusting his tongue into her mouth.

Deep inside her core came alive again, that lovely spiraling feeling rising once more. Below, at the entrance to her sex, something thick and hard nudged against her tender flesh. Alex moved, adjusted something down there, and the hardness pressed toward her opening. "Are you ready, sweetheart?"

Emma didn't think she was, but this was no time for cowardice. "Yes."

With a low groan, Alex pushed forward. The pressure grew and grew, then a burning streak made her cry out. The burn spread all throughout her nether regions before it began to subside. Meanwhile, Alex surged forward, thrusting home until his member lay deep inside her.

Emma lay panting, trying to discern how much hurt there actually was. The initial pain had been sharp, but it hadn't lasted long. Now there was only a dull ache all over. Was this all there was to it? Alex had said there would be more pleasure.

"Are you all right, Emma?" He peered into her face, his gaze darting here and there, concern in his eyes.

"I think so. Mostly, at least." She looked back at him, unsure if she should ask him this question or not. "You said there would be more pleasure. Is this it?"

Her husband smiled and shook his head. "No, but if you give me a moment, I think I can give us both some more." He leaned down and kissed her. As he did so, he pulled his member out of her then thrust back in.

"Ahhh." The burning was back, but as Alex began to withdraw and thrust, again and again, the pain subsided as the pleasure began to take hold of her. In and out. The rhythm of the movement started her spiraling upward, taking her toward that pinnacle of pleasure that was so much more than she'd believed possible.

"Wrap your legs around me, darling." Alex's voice came out gravelly with need.

Immediately, Emma lifted her legs and crossed them over his slim hips and buttocks. The shift in position must have opened her even more, for on his next thrust, Alex slid deeper than before, filling her completely. He drew back and thrust again and again until they were pounding into one another, Emma spinning upward, higher and higher with each thrust until Alex gave a great cry and shoved himself into her just as her core exploded again, releasing wave after wave of the sharpest pleasure she'd ever known. A hot gush poured into her. Alex strained against her then withdrew, rolling onto his back next to her, gulping in air as though he couldn't get enough.

Emma lay back, her mind whirling, trying to remember everything that had just happened. They were truly man and wife now. A wide grin spread over her face.

"Penny for your thoughts, Mrs. Bancroft." Alex raised up on one elbow to gaze into her face.

"You can get them for free, my dear." She rolled up on her side until they were face to face. "I was just thinking that now you're well and truly mine. We are bound to one another. No one can ever take you from me."

"Or you from me, my dear." He pushed a strand of hair out of her sweaty face, then kissed her forehead. "They say you should begin as you mean to go forward and I think this is exactly the way we want to go on." Alex pressed a long, passionate kiss onto her lips. "Don't you agree?"

"Oh, I do, Captain Bancroft." She snuggled into his chest. "But when can we go on this way again?"

CHAPTER EIGHT

"DO YOU THINK you'll be home for dinner tonight, my dear?" Taking a last bite of toast slathered generously with marmalade, Emma tried again to engage her husband in conversation.

After enjoying her breakfast in bed the first few days of her marriage, she realized she rarely saw Alex. He'd reported to the regiment the Monday after their wedding, which she completely understood. Duty was duty whether one had just been married or not. Then he'd begun to miss dinner, however, and she saw him only late at night when he came to bed. Their intimate interludes were joyous moments spent together, after which Alex fell into a dead sleep. And even though passion was all well and good, Emma wanted more from her marriage. So, she decided to alter her routine.

By coming down to eat breakfast with Alex, Emma believed she'd have a better chance of conversing with him. They'd been married two weeks and Emma had learned no more about her husband than she'd known on her wedding day. Today, she was determined to learn more.

"Hmm?" Looking up from his newspaper, Alex met her eyes briefly and smiled. "What did you say, dear?"

"I asked if you would be home for dinner. I was hoping we might be able to spend some time together." She put on her best smile. "I wanted to talk to you about a little notion I had that we might give a dinner party next month for some of the officers in your regiment. The married officers, I mean." Emma had hit upon this scheme several days ago when she decided to pay calls on her friends. To her chagrin, the only people she could think of to call on were Augusta and Lady Tilbury. She'd met few other young ladies during her partial Season, so now she was at a severe loss for companionship. Coming up with the scheme to meet the other officers' wives was a happy stroke of genius.

"I'm sorry, my dear, I had meant to tell you earlier." He folded his paper and reached for his coffee. "There is a training exercise this week, field maneuvers outside the city, that will keep me away until Friday morning. But then I have an entire day I can devote to—Emma, what's the matter, sweetheart?"

"You will be gone for three nights?" Oh, God. She'd be left alone. Instantly, tears began trickling down her cheeks.

"Emma." He rose swiftly, came around to her side of the table, knelt, and put his arms around her. "Shhh, my dear. Yes, the exercises take place out in the field, but it's nothing to worry about."

Tears continued to flow, even though his arms around her were warm and comforting. Never had she thought after she married that Alex would have to leave her. "But I will be all by myself."

"Darling, you have six servants here with you, two of them strong men. This is a quiet neighborhood. You will be safe here, I promise you."

"I only feel safe when I'm with you." She leaned her face against his chest, hating her weakness, but unable to overcome it.

"That is nice to hear." He pulled back so he could see her face. "But not very practical when you are married to a military man. There may be times when I am called away for more than a few days. What will you do then?"

Wiping her eyes with the back of her hand, Emma sniffed and turned her pleading gaze on him. "I didn't think that would happen. You said I could follow the drum." She would do that too, wherever it took her. As long as she had Alex by her side. "Can I do that now?"

"No, little soldier, you cannot." He stood and pulled her up to stand in front of him, a glint of sternness in his eyes. "It's only for a few nights, Emma. Why are you so afraid of spending the nights alone here?"

It was on the tip of her tongue to tell him, but Emma paused long enough for the impulse to pass. She wanted no one to know of those horrifying days and nights in India. "I have never been alone, Alex. I've always had my parents or my aunt and uncle, Lord and Lady Tilney, or you to look after me. I'm afraid to be alone without a man for protection."

"So it doesn't have to be me then?" He looked at her, an eyebrow raised.

"What do you mean?"

"As long as you have a protector, you will not be upset if I am gone?"

"Well, of course I'd prefer to have my husband by my side." Emma didn't like where the conversation seemed to be going.

"But another man would do?" The stern look was back in his eyes.

Sighing, she nodded. "Yes, I suppose so."

"Then I will send a note to Aunt Lucinda asking if you can come stay with her and Uncle Jack for a few days." His mouth softened as he bent his head to kiss her brow. "You might like having the company."

The offer was tempting. Even though his aunt was several years older than Emma, she'd liked her very much after meeting her at the house party and wedding. But… "Hampshire is a long way to travel just for a couple of nights, my dear." Perhaps she could stay with Augusta instead, although Emma loathed inviting herself. Maybe she should tough it out here alone, although the very thought made her shiver. "I'm afraid it won't do, my dear."

"If my aunt and uncle were in Hampshire, I wouldn't have

mentioned it. You're correct, that would be too great a journey alone on a train for you to attempt for just a few days' stay." Alex pulled a strand of her chestnut hair from beneath her lacy cap and wound it around his finger. "But I received a note from Uncle Jack yesterday saying he and my aunt had come up to Town for a few weeks before the Little Season begins."

"You didn't tell me that." This put a whole new light on the scheme.

He chuckled and dipped his head to whisper in her ear, "That is because you fell asleep immediately after we had our bit of jam last night, so I didn't have the chance to tell you."

"You could have told me before we…" Emma's face heated. She shouldn't be so embarrassed still about having marital congress, but she was. "Before we did it."

"I might have, my love, had you not been looking so delicious lying there in bed." He kissed the sensitive part of her neck just below her ear. "You can't expect me to think of anything other than having a game in the cock-loft when you lie there inviting me in."

Emma drew back, staring him down. "Well, I suppose there'll be no gaming of any kind tonight, will there?"

Alex sighed. "Unfortunately not."

"Then by all means, send a note to Aunt Lucinda and ask if I may stay with them." His cavalier manner about the matter made the devil fly into Emma. Serve him right if he didn't get any "jam" for several nights. "If she's willing, ask if I might stay until Saturday."

"Saturday?" Her husband's face drooped. Today was only Tuesday.

"I think you're right. I would like some feminine companionship." Now perhaps Alex would see how much he'd been neglecting her. "We see each other so seldom these days, I'd like to have someone to talk to about something other than…mundane topics."

"Very well, my dear." Alex stepped back, his gaze taking her in from top to toe. "I will write to her at once and send it by James. I'll direct her to send the answer to you. I expect it will arrive by lunch time."

"Excellent. I'll instruct Cooper to begin packing." She'd finally hired a lady's maid, and not a moment too soon. "I will see you on Saturday then."

Alex looked at her, his forlorn face making him look like a little boy, and Emma's heart gave a hitch. This was their first quarrel and the first time they had been apart since they wed. She didn't wish for them to part in anger. Raising up on tiptoe, she kissed his cheek. "Please be careful out in the wilds."

"Hampstead Heath is hardly the wilds, my dear." He smiled grudgingly, his good mood restored. "But I will take care to come back in one piece."

"Thank you." With a little toss of her head, she gave him a teasing smile and left the breakfast room. It might do her husband a great deal of good for them to be away from one another for a few days. Absence made the heart grow fonder, or so they said. And she wanted Alex to be fonder of her.

Emma started up the staircase, her thoughts whirling. She and Alex had been completely amicable, at least until this morning. Something in his demeanor, however, gave her the feeling that now that they were settled into married life, he was content for them to simply remain friends. Intimate friends, of that there was no doubt, but merely friends nonetheless. That seemed to be enough for him, and at one point, it would have been for her as well.

Living with Alex during the past two weeks, however, Emma had come to desire more from her marriage. Her feelings toward her husband had changed from simply wanting security. Now she wanted his feelings to deepen toward her, just as hers had toward him. Unfortunately, she didn't know how to make that happen. Perhaps talking with Aunt Lucinda might help in that regard. Her marriage to Uncle Jack seemed idyllic in the extreme. Emma would get her alone and beg her for that secret. Now that her safety had been secured, Emma found, to her surprise, she wished to settle for no less than a love match. No matter what it took. She would work hard toward that goal. And make sure Alex did too.

"I'D QUITE FORGOTTEN how bad field rations were, Bancroft. It's surprising how discerning one becomes when one marries." Captain Macauley leaned back in his chair, tipping up a glass of reasonably good burgundy. "The beef was too salty, the potatoes mealy, and the bread hard as ship's biscuits. I swear I never noticed such things before I married Jane. The cook she engaged is a culinary artist of the first water."

"I think I must agree with you, Mac." Alex picked at the tasteless potatoes, remembering his excellent meal last evening with a much more attractive dinner partner. "Our cook, Mrs. Parker, has outdone herself with each succeeding meal since my bride and I took up residence. We will be quite bereft when we have to move houses." Taking up the wine bottle, Alex refilled his glass. "For once, I don't look forward to the regiment's next assignment if it takes us out of England."

"Because you'll have to leave your cook behind?" Mac chuckled and finished his glass.

"That is one consideration, certainly." Laughing, Alex took up his glass. "A more important one is my wife. She was beside herself today when I told her the regiment was going into the field. Didn't want me to leave her." He shook his head. He'd no idea Emma would take his absence so hard. "I had to send her off to stay with my aunt and uncle."

"She's that skittish? But of course you're still newlyweds. New brides can be rather clingy in my experience." Producing a cigar, Mac leaned back and struck a match. "I wouldn't worry about it. We're not due to ship out until after Christmas. Mrs.

Bancroft will be a regular trooper by then."

Alex shook his head. "I don't know about that. Not after this morning. Have you heard anything about where we'll be going?" If they were sent to some easy posting, to France, say, or Belgium, then the move would be easy enough for Emma.

"Canada is the place I've heard most often bandied about, although someone mentioned India as well." Striking a match on the bottom of his boot, Mac lit his cigar. A haze of sweet smoke soon hovered around his head.

Alex's pulse quickened. Stories he'd heard of that exotic country had made him long all the more to be stationed there. "Ah, now India would be a bit of luck. I've been longing to be sent there ever since we came back from the Crimea." Would his wife share his enthusiasm, however? She'd just come from the Orient and might not fancy a return trip so soon. "What will your wife think of such a move?"

"Jane's used to following the drum. She'll take it in her stride." Mac took a puff and exhaled, sending the bluish smoke swirling into the peak of their tent. "The woman is so unwavering in her devotion to me, she would have followed us to the Crimea if I'd have let her. I insisted she stay with her mother, of course, and it's a good thing too."

"Damn right about that." Alex shuddered at the thought of Emma anywhere near a battlefield. "After our row this morning, I may not have to worry about her agreeing to come with us wherever we go."

"Nonsense, Bancroft. This little tiff will blow over once you get back to your snug little house." Mac gave him a knowing look.

"She claims I've been neglecting her…outside the bedchamber," he hastened to add when Mac's eyebrows shot upward. "And I confess, once we married and I took up my duties again, I backslid into my bachelor days." He spun the wineglass in his fingers. "Out drinking after hours, playing cards until late at night. Perhaps I do need to change my ways a bit. Pay her more attention."

"Once we're off maneuvers, why not take her to the Albion for dinner?" Mac tapped his ash into his plate. "I took Jane there for a special treat one evening. I'll tell you, she enjoyed it immensely." He leaned back and blew a smoke ring toward the roof. "Very appreciative she was, if you know what I mean."

Alex could imagine. "That sounds like a splendid idea, Mac. I'll contact them directly when we return."

"I will warn you, you may not get in very quickly. It's very popular with the East India Company nabobs as well as the upper echelon of the military. But you should be able to manage it by the first of the year."

"That won't do then." Alex needed a plan he could implement by this Saturday when Emma returned. "I'll call 'round there and see if I can get us seated, but if not, I'm still stuck for an idea how to make it up to Emma."

"If it's short notice, but you really wish to apologize, have your cook prepare a special meal." His friend took another long drag on his whiff and sent three smoke rings wafting. "Have her fix all her favorite dishes, or something extra special and fancy. A dinner of nothing but French dishes, perhaps." He kissed his fingertips. "*Ooh-la-la!*"

"That's not a bad idea, old chap." Leaning back in his chair, the scene began to take place in Alex's imagination. He'd make all the arrangements with Mrs. Parker in advance. Buckleigh would have the table set as for the grandest dinner party, only for two. Alex would make sure he made every effort to wait on her himself, initiate the conversation, keep her apprised of everything that had gone on during these few days they'd been apart and give her ample time to describe her visit with Aunt Lucinda. "I think this may prove the very thing to get me back into my wife's good graces—and her bed."

"She likes French food that much, does she?" Leering, Mac twirled the stub of his cigar in his fingers.

"Oh no. Not French. But you have put me in mind of something I'm certain she's going to love." Brilliant thought, genius in fact. He had the plan almost complete in his mind. Now all he need do was make arrangements with the cook and let nature take its course. Alex smiled broadly, sipping his wine as he plotted how to woo his wife with food she would certainly love.

"THE CARRIAGE HAS just arrived, Captain Bancroft." The butler made the announcement from the door of the dining room.

"Excellent, thank you, Buckleigh." Alex cast a final look over the lavish table setting, silverware gleaming proudly in the candlelight. The air was filled with unusual but delicious aromas that made Alex's mouth water. He tugged at his uniform, wanting everything to be exactly right, then swiftly headed through the doorway toward the front of the house. He wanted to personally escort his wife in to their special dinner.

Emma had just been helped down to the pavement when he arrived at the carriage. The sight of her luscious figure, in a very seductive lowcut green and gold gown, almost took his breath away. His cock stirred immediately, bumping against his trousers with an urgency difficult to deny. Perhaps he should have put dinner off until later, until he and his wife had had the opportunity to reacquaint themselves in the bedroom. He hadn't thought this short time apart would affect him so badly. But dinner was almost ready, so he must carry forward and hope to quell his ardor for the present.

"My dear, you look absolutely ravishing." He leaned forward and gave her a kiss on the cheek. "I trust you had a good visit with Aunt Lucinda?"

"We did." She smiled up at him, her big blue eyes melting his heart. "It was good to be able to talk to other women for a change. I quite enjoyed myself."

"Other women?" He offered his arm and she took it eagerly,

twining her arm in his.

"Yes, Lucinda invited some of her friends to tea and introduced me. We all had such a lovely time, and now I have acquaintances I can call on in Town." Emma sounded so happy. Alex hadn't realized his wife had been lonely.

"That sounds splendid, my love. And when we have your dinner party for the married officers and their wives, you will have even more ladies to call upon." They had reached the front door, so Alex paused. "Speaking of dinner parties, I have arranged a special homecoming dinner just for you, Emma."

"Alex, how thoughtful of you." She rose up on tiptoe and kissed his lips, lingering just long enough to make him hungry in a very different way. "I know we parted on strained terms, but I am glad that is all in the past now. I so want us to have a good marriage, my love."

"As do I, sweetheart." He did want their union to be a success. Tonight should go a long way to making it so. "Here, let us go in, but let me ask you to shut your eyes."

The pools of blue widened. "But why?"

"The better to surprise you, my dear."

With a giggle, Emma nodded and dutifully closed her eyes.

Buckleigh opened the door and Alex helped Emma into the house. "This way, love."

The butler took her shawl, and Emma stepped further into the house, wrinkling her nose. "What is that smell?"

Alex grinned. "Does it seem familiar?"

"Yes, it does." She shrank back against him. "I don't like this, Alex. Can I open my eyes now?"

"Let me take you to the dining room, then you can open them." He steered her down the corridor to the threshold of the room. "Now you can open them, love."

He stepped back, wanting the best view of her face when she saw how he'd transformed their normal dining room into his idea of an Indian palace. The walls were draped with colorful gauzy fabric, caught up at intervals with ribbons. Instead of the normal tablecloth, red cloth shot with gold covered the table where all the best crystal and china were laid. Spread out over the bright expanse lay all manner of Indian dishes Mrs. Parker had managed to find recipes for or adapted from her own. Crisp vegetable fritters, creamy curried vegetables, lamb in a spicy red sauce, flatbread, and fragrant rice. The sight and smell of the unusual dishes made Alex hungry.

About to ask Emma if she was surprised, Alex frowned to see her staring at the room, her nose flaring, her body trembling, her face drained of color. "Emma, what's wrong?"

Her head started to shake from side to side, gaining momentum as she began backing toward the door. "No…no…no!"

"Emma?" Alex had no idea what had come over his wife. He took her arm, but she threw it off, whirling toward him.

"No! No!" Tears dripped down her agonized face. "I can't… Not again."

"What is wrong, my dear?" Alex grasped her arm—she looked so ghastly he feared she might swoon.

With a strength he didn't believe possible from her, Emma pulled free, gave him one stricken look, then bolted from the room.

CHAPTER NINE

SOBBING NEARLY HYSTERICAL tears, Emma fled up the stairs, taking some of them two at a time. She had to get away, go hide herself so no one could find her. Throwing the door open so forcefully it banged into the wall behind it, Emma ran for the far side of the bed and dove underneath it without a thought for either her clothes or her body. She banged her head on the underside of the bed, but ignored the sharp pain and continued to burrow underneath it.

Were those footsteps in the hall? She froze, listened closely, then continued to squeeze herself into the smallest ball she could and waited, trying not to whimper. That pungent aroma wafted over her, filling her nose with the nasty smell until she wanted to stuff her nose with something to block it out.

The steps grew slower. Oh, she should have closed and locked the door. Now she must be absolutely silent so they couldn't find her.

"Emma?"

She stiffened, scarcely breathing.

"Emma, where are you, sweetheart?" The soft voice seemed familiar.

The steps came closer until she could see the black shoes from under the bed. Then a concerned face appeared. "Emma, what are you doing under there?"

Alex. He'd come to rescue her. "Alex," she whispered. "Thank God. Please, please, take me away from here."

He frowned but nodded. "Of course I will, darling. Can you come out from under the bed?" His face disappeared. "Then we can go."

She didn't want to move for fear the sepoys would find her. But this was Alex. He wouldn't let anyone hurt her. Summoning all her courage, she inched toward the edge of the bed. The horrid scent seemed to intensify as she moved toward more open air. Gorge rose in her throat, but she bit it back. She'd be out of here soon. Alex would take her. He'd keep her safe.

At last she steeled her nerve and poked her head out from under the bed.

Alex stood there, peering down on her, a tender look in his eyes. "Give me your hand, my love. I'll help you up."

"And then we'll go?" They had to escape.

"If you wish it, yes."

She wished it more than anything in the world.

He held out his hand and she took it. Gently, he drew her out from under the bed until she stood before him, his eyes terribly kind. "Come, my dear, sit quietly here for a moment." He steered her to the pretty little chaise in front of the fireplace and sat her down. "Now, you rest here—"

"No, no, Alex, you can't leave me!" She grabbed his arm and held on. "They will take me if you leave." She clung to him, unable to release her iron grip on his arm.

"Dearest, there is no one here to harm you." As he spoke softly, he rubbed her shoulders then dropped a kiss on her forehead. But his eyes were worried. "Are you having some sort of waking dream? About your stay in India? I assure you, you are safe here in England. No one is going to harm you."

Cautiously, Emma sought his eyes. Her husband wouldn't lie about such things. "We're in England?"

"In the very heart of London, my love."

Glancing around the room, Emma's shoulders slumped. Her

mind cleared of the frantic fog that had enveloped it and she took a deep breath. "Yes, this is England. This is our house, our room." As she spoke it was as if everything around her came back into focus. She was safe, now and for always, with Alex by her side. "Oh, Alex." She launched herself into his arms, hugging him fiercely. "I am so sorry."

"You have nothing to be sorry for, love." He put her gently from him to peer into her face. "Can you tell me what happened just now? Why you ran away? Who or what were you hiding from?"

She hid her face in her hands, regretting that she hadn't told him what had happened before now. Well, time to pay the piper. "Yes, I need to tell you what happened to me. To us."

He stepped to the door and rang the bell. "We'll have some tea. It will do you good against this shock. You mean to your aunt and uncle? Out in India?"

Emma nodded. She'd never wanted to think about their ordeal ever again, but her lunatic behavior just now told her that hiding from the truth had not been in her best interest. Perhaps facing it, confessing it to Alex, would somehow exorcise the demons that still haunted her, both in her dreams and in her waking hours as well. She raised her head to gaze into the worried eyes of her husband. "It wasn't always a nightmare, you know? When we first arrived in Bombay, the country was like a fairy tale to me. I was just fourteen, a very impressionable young lady, and thought the entire trip a great adventure."

"I can just imagine." Alex took her hand and chaffed it between his.

"We spent much of the first year in Oudh, some of it in the palace of the ruler, Wajid Ali Shah." That had been a wonderful time for her, seeing everything fresh and new. "After that, my uncle toured around the provinces on business for the East India Company. I never knew what he did other than talk to different Indian rulers or British generals and other East Indian stock holders. We were visiting one of them in Sitapur in 1857 when the mutiny broke out."

Emma squeezed his hand and Alex squeezed back. "Take your time, my love. We have all the time in the world."

She gazed up at him, trying with all her heart to convince herself that was true. "When news of the uprising reached us, we were fairly alarmed, but my uncle and Mr. Jonas, who we were visiting, received instructions for us all to remove to the Residency in Lucknow, a little more than fifty miles away. We traveled in a small cart pulled by bullocks and it took the better part of a week, all during which we became more and more frightened of the uprising that was occurring all around us."

The door opened and Emma jumped up, but it was only James with the tea tray.

"Don't be alarmed, my dear. Thank you, James. You can set it just there." Alex indicated a little table nearest him. "And can you ask Buckleigh to make certain all the dinner is taken away? There should not be a single piece of it left in the house. The servants are welcome to it, but it must all be gone before morning."

"Very good, Captain." James bowed and made to leave, but Alex stopped him.

"Tell Mrs. Parker to thoroughly clean the room and remove all traces of the decorations." Alex looked at Emma thoughtfully. "And make very certain the smell of the food is gone. I don't care if you have to burn feathers to take away the odor. I want no trace of the dinner lingering at all."

"Yes, Captain. I will tell her immediately." The footman bowed again and scurried out.

"Go on, my dear. I will pour the tea." Alex gave a little nod and lifted the teapot.

Bless her husband. By some miracle, he seemed to understand rather than blame her for her bizarre behavior. Her knight in regimentals. "Well, once we arrived at the Residency, around the middle of June, we discovered they'd been besieged for almost three weeks." The beginning of the siege seemed like a party compared to the ending of it. "We were assigned a small room in the Residency, with decent rations at first, and there was some occupation with talking with the other women seeking refuge there."

"It doesn't sound bad to begin with," Alex paused to hand her some tea, "but I expect you were terribly anxious. Not knowing what to do, how to protect yourselves."

Emma's hand began to shake and she set her cup down on the table, her tea untasted. "There was no way to protect us, Alex. The Residency hadn't been built to withstand the punishment of the guns and mines. We kept out of the most exposed areas, but the enemy's guns seemed to find some people regardless." Tears trickled down her face and she swallowed hard. "One bullet found my uncle, sitting in a chair near the window in our room." She could see his face so clearly even now. "One moment he was talking to us, trying to assure us that Sir Henry Lawrence would see us through this ordeal, and the next he was slumped in his chair, a bullet in his neck."

"Emma." Without a moment's pause, Alex had slid next to her, put his arms around her shoulders, and hugged her to him. "Shhh, love. I'm so sorry. Don't speak of this if it distresses you so. You've endured enough today."

"No, Alex, I must tell you. I should have told you about this before we married." To be held close to his chest gave Emma the most comfort she'd had in days. "You should have known."

"Why didn't you tell me?" He kissed her forehead, and she relaxed a trifle.

"I was afraid if you knew I'd been there during the mutiny, you'd want nothing to do with me. You'd think I'd be damaged in some horrible way." Emma pressed her face against his broad chest, calmed by the wonderful masculine feel of him. "Which I am."

"Nonsense." He pulled her closer, the barest hint of his sandalwood cologne soothing her frayed senses. "You were undoubtedly courageous to have born the depravations of the siege so long and so well."

"Not well at all, Alex." Shaking her head, she tried to bury herself deeper against him. "I was afraid constantly. I tried not to let my aunt know, but she did. We were all more and more frightened as the siege wore on and our defenses weakened. Soldiers died every day. The enemy shelled the structure and blew up mines almost daily, undermining the Residency walls themselves."

The wall of flames she dreamed about so often sprang up before her eyes. "One night, one shell from the enemy hit the wall near where my aunt and I were sleeping. It caught the bedclothes on fire. In moments, my aunt was in flames." She hugged Alex, praying for the image of her aunt screaming to subside. When he squeezed her tighter, some of the fear and horror receded. "I have nightmares to this day about that."

"My love, I wish you would have shared this with me." He spoke low, directly into her ear, the warmth of his breath easing her misery a trifle. "I could have helped you when you were afraid."

"You would?" That offer was sweeter than any she'd ever had.

"Of course I would." He began to rock her gently, the slight swaying motion surprisingly calming. "We are as one, remember? I will always do whatever is in my power to help you and to keep you from harm." Alex pulled back and lifted her face to his. "You believe me, don't you, sweetheart?"

Gazing into his deep blue eyes, Emma couldn't help but believe him. Alex was so strong, so kind, so dutiful. If he promised to protect her, she understood he would lay down his life for her if need be. Who could not believe such a man? Who could not love such a one?

Emma gasped and sat back. She'd never allowed herself to think such a thing about Alex. They were amicable, they were good companions, they were passionate toward one another in the nighttime. He'd given her the deepest sense of safety she'd known since her return to England. But above all this, had she actually fallen in love with her husband?

"Do you believe me, Emma?" His gaze bore straight to her soul. "Do you?"

"I do, Alex." She grasped his hands, not ever wanting to let go. "I do believe you, my dear."

"Then tell me the rest of your ordeal so we may put it all behind you."

If only she could. After living with the nightmare for so long, she couldn't imagine a time she'd not lived in fear. But she could try. With a sigh, she straightened and continued. "There's not a lot left to tell, except the normal things one endures during a siege. The privations of food and any other creature comforts, the constant fighting, the deaths due to the enemy and to the diseases that ran rampant in the compound. The rats." These were some of the hardest things. Yet she'd not had to endure the ultimate devastation. "The deaths of so many children. Scarcely a woman with little ones escaped having to bury one of their darlings. By the time we were relieved, I believe I was completely numb to any emotion." She raised her long neglected tea to her lips. It was stone cold, but she didn't mind. She needed to finish the story. "That is why it took me so long to return to England. Once the Residency was relieved—the second time, mind you. The first relief effort couldn't actually relieve us but joined our forces. But once we were truly rescued, we started out on our journey to Calcutta in November, landing there after many different changes of conveyance in February of 1858."

"That was over two years ago, my dear." Alex had raised his teacup, but paused and frowned. "Why did you not sail for England immediately?"

"Most of the women who had come from the Residency did take ship almost as soon as we arrived. But I..." Emma looked away. "By the time I arrived in Calcutta, I wasn't quite myself. I kept thinking I was back at the Residency, that we were still under siege." She raised her gaze to his. "You've seen how that looks. It was even worse two years ago. The doctors at the garrison didn't know what to do with me. Fortunately, they were able to contact one of my uncle's friends living in the city. He and his wife took me in until I had come more to my senses and was able to sail for England." She shrugged. "You know the rest from there."

"I do." He looked deeply into her eyes. "And I am more grateful now that you are my wife than I have ever been."

"You are?" Those had not been the words she'd expected to hear from him. "You don't wish you needn't put up with me and all my lunacies?"

"Far from it, my love." Alex pulled her back to him. "I know now how strong you truly are. To have survived such an ordeal shows me that you are exactly the kind of strong, capable woman I'd want as my wife. I'm sorry that I made you recall that nightmare, and I only hope you can forgive me. Lesson learned. From today, we'll move on together, both of us stronger for having gone through the experience. Can we do that, Emma?"

An unimaginable weight lifted from Emma's shoulders and she threw her arms around Alex, hugging him so tightly she feared she might hurt him. But she was so very grateful for this magnificent man who could accept her with all her faults and still wish to be married to her. Who wouldn't love such a man? "Yes, my love. We absolutely can."

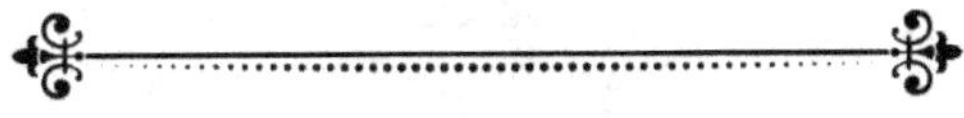

Chapter Ten

TWO DAYS AFTER Emma's astounding revelation, Alex arranged to meet Uncle Jack at the Rum Pum-Pas Club, a boxing establishment owned by James Langham, the current middleweight boxing champion. Alex and his uncle had sparred for years, his uncle having taken a liking to the sport as a young man. Although he didn't often fancy getting trounced, as he so often was by his enthusiastic uncle, this morning Alex was willing to take his drubbing in order to be able to talk to his uncle about a matter that had been on his mind over the weekend.

Jack entered the Cambrian Stores, Langham's tavern over which the boxing club sat, and hurried up the stairs. As he approached the entrance, the dull thudding blows of bare-knuckles on bare flesh reached him, punctuated by the guttural grunts of two pugilists in the midst of a match. He walked through the doorway just as a hefty-looking bloke landed a right hook to his young opponent's nose. Blood flew in a spectacular arc and the chap sank to his knees then crashed forward onto the mat.

"Alex." His uncle stood to the side of the ring, chest bared, ready for their turn in the ring. For a man forty-nine years of age, Uncle Jack was still a fine specimen of a man. Barrel-chested, powerful shoulders, and long arms. Sometimes it was difficult for Alex to land a blow on him at all.

"Good morning, uncle. I see you're fit and ready for action." Alex doffed his jacket and pulled his cravat free. "When do we go?"

"There's one more sparring round before us." He nodded as two assistants helped the young chap with blood trickling down off his chin out of the ring. "Depending on who it is, we may have some time." His uncle peered at him thoughtfully. "You said you wanted to talk to me about something important."

"I do." With a practiced motion, Alex pulled his shirt over his head and tossed it onto the chair holding his growing pile of clothes. Giving his arms a few good swings to help him limber up, Alex cast an eye over the crowded scene. Gentlemen in all stages of undress milled around, betting on various rounds, chatting, smoking. Hardly the setting for an intimate conversation, but Alex didn't want to wait and his uncle had given this time as his only free moments that day. "It's about Emma."

"Your wife?" Uncle Jack looked taken aback. "I thought you wanted my advice on buying some new cattle or an estate for your new home." He eyed Alex, frowning. "Is she well?" His brows rose sharply. "Is she already in a family way?"

"No, I mean, yes. I mean…" Alex had to stop himself from blithering away as his uncle's face became more excited.

"By Jove, well done, nephew." He slapped Alex on the shoulder, making him wince. "You've won another wager, I'll be bound. This is marvelous news. Our sons will be almost of an age, so I'm certain they'll be the best of friends."

"Wait a moment, uncle, before congratulating me." He managed to stop the flow of the older man's enthusiasm. "What I meant was yes, Emma is in good health, but no, she's not 'in the pudding club,' as they say. At least not yet, or not that I know." That brought up an even more pressing reason for his conversation. He must soldier on with this. "I wanted to ask you how you know when you love a woman."

"How do you know…*what*?" His uncle looked appalled. "Why would you ask me that?"

"Because you and Aunt Lucinda seem to be in love, uncle. From all that I can tell when I've seen you together. You dote on her and she on you. You both seem supremely happy whenever you're together." He was making a muddle of this and that wouldn't do. "Isn't that love?"

His uncle stepped back and stared at him thoughtfully. "Yes, yes, it is. At least as far as I'm concerned, it is. I just never thought about it like that before."

"So when did you know, uncle? When did you know you loved her?" After Emma's confession the other night, Alex had noticed a change in his manner toward his wife. He'd been gentler with her, kinder. More attentive. Each time he thought of her ordeal in India, his protective instincts made him want to go to her, hold her in his arms, and reassure her that no one would ever hurt her like that again. Was this love or just the normal instincts a gentleman had whenever he was able to provide protection for a lady, no matter who she was? "When?"

"I think from the first moment I saw Lucinda, I loved her. At least a little."

That made sense to Alex. He'd had that instant attraction to Emma, standing there on the stairs, the most beautiful lady he'd ever seen. So perfect and lovely he couldn't take his eyes off her. "I know what you mean, uncle. I couldn't stop staring at Emma when I first saw her at your party."

"Is this about Emma?" His uncle frowned. "Don't you know if you love her or not?"

Caught out, all Alex could do was hang his head. "No, I don't. I've never been in love before."

There was a ruckus in the ring. Alex looked up to see both combatants on the floor, the one on top pounding the other one for all he was worth. "Tell me what the signs are, Uncle Jack. I feel so strange when I'm around her."

"You're going to feel something else strange in a minute, Alexander, and I can promise you it won't be love. Let's move over to the ropes. It won't be long—"

"Lord Caxton? This way, my lord." One of Langham's instructors motioned to them, and Alex followed his uncle into the ring. Alex had begun to dread this match even more than usual. His uncle seemed to be displeased with him, and when Uncle Jack was unhappy with a person, that person knew it in no uncertain terms.

"Five rounds in the bout today, gentlemen." The instructor raised his hand.

Quickly, Alex assumed the usual position, his raised fists forming a guard for his face.

"Begin."

Whap.

Alex's head snapped back as Uncle Jack's fist found its way directly to his jaw. He managed to parry the next few blows, then struck out with his own, which was neatly blocked. Alex shook it off, then commenced dancing around, just out of his uncle's reach. "So tell me what I'm supposed to feel, uncle. If I'm in love with Emma?"

"Hard to say, old chap." Uncle Jack moved in like a flash, aiming for Alex's jaw again.

This time, he managed to avoid the blow and landed a lucky one to his uncle's chin. The older man staggered back.

"Try to say, uncle." There was no one else he could consult on this. His cousins hadn't been in love, he'd never ask his grandfather this sort of question. And Harry was still off on his blasted honeymoon. Uncle Jack was the closest thing he'd had to a father in years. Alex would have the answer if he had to beat it out of him. "I need to know if I'm in love with her or not."

"I never had to ask anyone, nephew. I just knew." Uncle Jack bobbed and weaved around the ring, Alex following, looking for his next advantage. "Whenever Lucinda entered a room, I couldn't take my eyes off her. If she left a room, it was like the sun had set even though it was mid-day."

Alex tried a feint to the left, then countered with his right, but his opponent was too wily. Another sharp pain to his left eye and Alex could barely see out of it. "So you always wanted to be around her, never wanted to leave her alone?"

"I still do. But we don't wish to live on one another's pockets, so we make that sacrifice occasionally, like this morning, to be with others that we love as well." Uncle Jack began a series of punishing blows to Alex's face, which Alex could scarcely fend off. Where did the man get his stamina? "But I'm on fire every moment we're apart. I cannot wait until I'm with her again. Like there's an emptiness inside me that can only be filled by her presence."

Out of nowhere, Uncle Jack sank his fist into Alex's stomach, knocking the wind out of his lungs and sending him thumping onto his back on the floor. As he lay there trying to coax his lungs to accept air once more, his uncle came to stand over him, peering down at him with a grin on his face.

"That sensation you're feeling right now, Alex, that emptiness in your stomach when the wind's been knocked out of you and you never saw it coming? That's what falling in love is like. At least it was for me. Lucinda can bring me to my knees with one hurt glance. There's nothing I wouldn't do for her. If that's what you're feeling when you look at Emma, well then," he reached down, grasped Alex's hand, and helped him to his feet, "welcome to the club, nephew. You're in excellent company now."

"DOES UNCLE JACK always give you this severe a drubbing when you play at fisticuffs?"

Alex winced as Emma dabbed at the cut over his eye with a cloth soaked in witch hazel. The astringent stung, but not as much as his wife's words had ever since he'd arrived home and presented his bruised face. "He usually bests me, I'll admit that. He's had years more practice than I have. But today he seemed…a little annoyed at me." That was putting it mildly. "I think he took that annoyance out on my face."

"Well, I think that is awful. He shouldn't have been so mean-spirited." His wife sat back on the chaise. As soon as she'd seen his bruised and swelling face, she'd brought him directly to their bedchamber and called for warm water and several remedies. "What on earth did you ask him to make him treat you so?"

Well, he'd been expecting that question. "It was something of a personal nature."

"A personal question? About what?"

An inquisitive wife was the bane of any husband with something to hide. But he wouldn't lie to her. "About Aunt Lucinda."

Emma's brow wrinkled and her eyes narrowed. "What did you want to know about Lucinda that would be so personal he'd do this to you?"

Whoever said honesty was the best policy was surely a bachelor. Alex took a deep breath. "I wanted to know how it felt when they fell in love."

"Oh." Emma sat back on the chaise, the cloth clutched in her hand. She looked at him, blinking rapidly. "Why would you wish to know that?"

Such declarations should not be made in such a prosaic manner, but in for a penny... He took her hand and squeezed it. "Because I have never been in love before, so I wanted to know if what I was feeling when I looked at you was love."

Her eyes widened and she gripped his hand as though it were a lifeline. "A...and is it?"

"Oh yes." He leaned forward to press a kiss on her trembling lips. "I believe it is."

"Oh, Alex." With a little gasp, she threw her arms around his neck, hugging him tightly, pressing her breasts against his chest until he could swear he could feel her nipples hardening against him. That couldn't be real, not through the armor of her corset, but in his imagination, he could feel them brushing his flesh, making his member harden just from the image.

He rose, catching her up in his arms and bringing her to her feet as well.

"Oh, Alex." She gazed into his face, her eyes glistening with unshed tears and joy. "I love you too. So very much." Pulling his head down to her, she peppered his face and lips with quick, darting little kisses that made his cock frantic.

There was nothing else for it. He scooped her up and strode to the bed, made to toss her onto it and then follow, but looked down at her dress, stymied. "Damn, we wear too many clothes."

Giggling, Emma wiggled herself to the floor and turned around. "Unbutton me, please. Then I can do the rest."

That was a skill at which he was very adept. With speed born of great urgency, he pulled the fabric covered buttons out of their loops in record time. As soon as the dress began to sag, Emma pulled it out of his hands. "You'd better start on your own clothes, my dear." She sent a sultry glance over her shoulder and his heart stopped. "You don't want to keep me waiting."

No, he did not. Alex pulled the cravat from his neck, almost choking himself in the process. His hands flew to his trousers, ripped the garment open, and pulled them and his drawers down to his boots. Drat. He hopped about, pulling first one then the other boot off, and kicked the clothing aside. Now unencumbered, his cock stood straight out, tenting his shirt in a rather comical way. But none of this was a laughing matter. He burned with an intensity hereto unknown to possess his wife's body, to show her irrevocably how much he adored her.

Glancing at the bed, Alex's breath stopped.

Naked, Emma lay on her side, one arm stretched out above her head, her other hand rubbing the cover in front in invitation. Never had she looked so utterly beautiful. "Come to bed, my love."

With one movement, Alex tore the shirt over his head, threw it into the air, and bolted for the bed. He sailed up onto it, pushed Emma onto her back, and covered her, unable to wait one moment more to feel her pressed against him, bare skin to bare skin. The exquisite warmth and softness of her body overwhelmed him, and he had to stifle the urge to immediately plunge into her. This time, he needed to show her how much he cared, that her pleasure was just as, if not more important, than his own.

"What would you like me to do, Emma?" He raised his head to gaze at her beautiful face.

With a throaty sigh, she said, "Make love to me, Alex."

"Of course, my love. But what exactly would you like me to do? Where do I start?"

Frowning, she raised her head up. "I…I don't know."

Lifting himself overtop of her, instantly bereft of the intense closeness he experienced when their bodies were joined, he touched his lips lightly to her neck. "Do you like that?"

"Yes." She smiled and closed her eyes.

"How about this?" Sliding his lips down to the base of her neck, he licked the skin, then massaged it with the tip of his tongue.

"Hmm, yes." She sighed, her hips restless beneath him.

"And this?" Alex moved to her breast, clasped his lips around her nipple, and sucked gently.

"Ohhh, yesss." The change in her voice to a guttural tone would have been enough to excite Alex, but she thrust her hips against his member, still standing at attention, as if seeking him out.

Groaning, Alex flicked his tongue over her nipple until it tightened into a hard point. Oh, he longed to sink himself into her hot sheath, but tonight was about what she wanted, not him. Gently, he closed his teeth around her peak and slowly scraped them across her tender flesh.

Emma's low moan almost undid him, but he carried on, licking and sucking on her breast, rubbing himself against her nether regions until her shallow panting made him pause. "Darling, what do you want me to do now?"

"Oh, take me, Alex. Take me now." She opened her thighs and wrapped her legs around him, resting her heels on his bare buttocks.

"Are you certain that's what you want?" He'd believed she'd want more love play.

Her reply was to press her heels down and squeeze his cock against her nest of soft curls.

Alex needed no further invitation. Swiftly, he guided himself to her opening then plunged in, almost spilling himself there and then. Just barely, he pulled himself back from the brink—he wanted to make certain she achieved her pleasure before he did—then began a slow-moving rhythm designed to bring her to the pinnacle. "Do you like that, sweetheart?"

"So much, Alex. It feels wonderful—oh!"

He'd changed the rhythm for a moment, pumping hard and deep before returning to the steady thrusts. "And that?"

"Don't tease me." She pushed her hips up against him just as he drove forward, making him slip deeper into her hot channel. "Oh, yes, yes. Do that again."

If he did, it would be all over. Alex snaked his hand down, found her mons and the little pearl inside it. Swirling his finger around the sensitive little nub, he pulled back then slid deeper again and again.

"Alex, oh, my love. Yes." She clasped her arms around his neck, her hips slapping against his until, with a low moan, she shattered.

As her sheath throbbed around him, Alex thrust again, emitted his own bellow, and spent himself deep inside her. Joy and relief shot throughout him as he pumped once more, then stilled, hovering above Emma, propped up on his elbows. The glow of happiness on her face gave him almost as much satisfaction as the release he'd just achieved. Almost. He leaned down and kissed her lips, then rolled to the side and lay panting beside her.

Strange as it was, his thoughts strayed back to his bout with Uncle Jack and the gut punch that had laid him low. His uncle had been wrong, however. His feelings for Emma had nothing to do with emptiness, and everything to do with fulfilment. His cup of happiness was overflowing, and the sole reason was the woman lying next to him, a light sheen of sweat glistening on her beautiful body. If this was love—and he was now certain it was—he had to be the luckiest man alive. And he'd spend the rest of his life making certain Emma was the happiest woman.

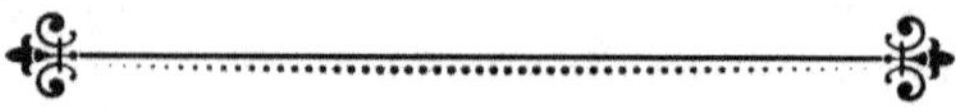

Chapter Eleven

"Where are we going?" Emma peered out of the carriage window as the residential sections of London gave way to more mercantile establishments.

"I'm so sorry about that dinner you…didn't enjoy that I wanted to make it up to you." Alex took her gloved hand, pressing a kiss to the back of it. "I thought I'd do that by taking you out to dinner this time."

Her eyes grew round. "An evening at a restaurant. How lovely, my dear. I've never eaten at a restaurant in public."

"Well, we won't actually be in public. I had to engage a private room, but I still thought it would be a treat." It had taken him some time to find an eating establishment that would allow his wife to dine with him. Not being in the company of ladies overly much, he'd not realized women weren't welcomed into most restaurants.

"But where are we going?" Emma leaned forward, looking from side to side.

"The Albion Tavern. Despite its name, it's got quite a good reputation for both its food and the elegance of its rooms." He certainly hoped it would live up to the extravagant recommendation he'd gotten from Mac. It had taken a solid month to reserve the room, and only after Uncle Jack had stepped in and put a flea in the manager's ear. Having a peer as one's relation often helped one along in life.

The carriage pulled to a halt in front of a wide brick and stone building front that towered four stories high. Alex jumped down to the sidewalk, the sharp November wind whistling by his ears. He handed his wife down and waited while she craned her neck to marvel at the building's height before looping her arm through his and making quickly for the columned entryway.

A maître d' opened the door and ushered them in amidst a blast of wintry air. "Good evening." He took in Emma then glanced quickly to Alex. "Captain Bancroft, it is a pleasure to see you, sir. Your room is this way, if you will follow me."

They moved swiftly through the main dining room, table after table of gentlemen eating heartily. Many of them, however, paused their conversations or suspended their dinners to stare at Emma as she passed by them. Blast, but he didn't want her to feel like a beast in a zoo or a freak in a circus side show. Again, he'd not thought this through enough. He glanced at his wife, who didn't seem overly upset, but had a slight smile on her lips. He'd have to ask her about that once they were out of the public eye.

Finally, they arrived at a series of doors and the maître d' opened the one on the far left. Alex quickly ushered Emma inside, thankful to be out of sight of the other diners at last.

"Your waiter will be with you shortly, Captain Bancroft." The maître d' bowed and left, closing the door behind him.

"I'm so sorry about that, sweetheart." Alex turned to Emma, who was gazing about the room, smiling broadly.

"About what, my dear?" She peered up at the huge stag's head mounted over the roaring fireplace. "My, that's a big deer."

"The way the other diners were staring at you." Such a lack of manners was intolerable. "If it wouldn't have caused a ruckus, I'd have chastised them for their ill-breeding."

Emma strode over to him and took his arm, squeezing it tightly. "Always my hero. But I'm glad you didn't. We didn't need to be more of a spectacle than they already seemed to think I was."

"You are very kind to take it so well. I even saw you smiling."

She giggled, making her look even more beautiful. "I was thinking they must never have understood a woman would like to have a meal out with her husband. Their wives must be so sad." She gazed up at him and his stomach dropped at the love so apparent in her eyes. "My husband, however, knows what a wife likes very well."

"I certainly hope I do." He dipped down and kissed her lips. "Would you like some sherry before dinner? There's some on the sideboard there."

"See, you know exactly what a wife wants." With a flirtatious little lift to her eyebrows, Emma sat in one of the two leather arm chairs on either side of the fireplace.

The minx. If he didn't think it would get them thrown out of the Albion, he'd give his wife what she truly wanted. This was a private room after all. Of course, the waiter would be in soon. So, for now, the sherry would have to suffice. He poured the libation into two very pretty cut-crystal glasses and handed her one. "Bon appetite, my dear."

Emma raised her glass to him then sipped, her eyes closing slightly as she savored the wine. "Delicious."

Enveloped by the comfortable chair, the roaring fire beside her, her tiered silk gown of deep rose revealing her white shoulders and emphasizing her slender neck, Emma put him in mind of a rare jewel nestled on a soft cushion. Waiting to be plucked up and enjoyed to the fullest. "Delicious indeed."

Perhaps some of his desire showed too well, for her cheeks pinkened, and she sipped her sherry more frequently until the glass was drained. She set it on a nearby table and looked up at him, a slight seductive smile on her lips. "Now what should we do?"

Alex's fingers tightened on his glass. She must know damned well what he *wanted* to do. This evening had taken a strange turn, with his wife trying to tempt him to ravish her in a public place. Well, the room was private enough for a little dalliance except they were certain to be interrupted by the servers. Perhaps they might have a little time before—

A quick rap on the door and the waiter opened it, a large silver tray in his hands. "Turtle soup, sir."

"Thank you." He set his glass down and moved to Emma, offering his arm. "Let me assist you to the table, my dear."

Eyes demurely downcast—surely for the waiter's benefit as his wife didn't have a demure bone in her body—Emma took his arm and let him lead her to the table. Once he'd seated her, he sat down opposite her at the long dinner table that had been set for two. "You may serve now."

Once the steaming bowls were laid before them, the waiter hurried out, leaving them alone. The rich aroma of herbs and turtle made Alex's mouth water. He dipped his spoon in and soon was savoring the meaty goodness of the dish. "This is excellent."

"I agree." Emma spooned up the broth, popped it into her mouth, and smiled with satisfaction. "This course is certainly a lovely beginning to our evening." She stared straight into his eyes and licked her lips. "But I suspect it will pale in comparison to the dishes yet to come."

Alex's brows shot up. If his wife wished to be outrageous, then he would follow suit. "If you are correct, my dear, we will be truly sated by the time we reach home."

"I certainly hope so." Emma laughed, and they finished the soup with little talk but a great deal of sly looks.

The waiter returned shortly with a tray of savory pastries. "Oysters Bouchees, sir."

Alex met Emma's eyes. Her lips drew into a little pucker, as though she was trying not to laugh. He clenched his jaw to avoid the same thing. "Thank you," he managed to growl, and the servant hurried out. The door had scarcely closed before Alex could contain himself no longer. He laughed loudly, joined immediately by Emma's full-throated whoop.

"You ordered these on purpose, didn't you, Alex?" She wiped tears from her eyes then settled back in her chair and looked at him expectantly.

"I would love to take the credit, but I have to confess I did not." Alex continued to chuckle. "This must be part of the table d'hote—their regular fixed menu. I had nothing to do with it. Although," he grabbed the serving spoon and placed several of the little pastries on their plates, "I think we must take advantage of this serendipitous course." He eyed her lasciviously. "Don't you?"

"Oh, yes." Emma brought the pastry to her mouth and bit into it slowly. Some of the juice from the plump oyster squirted onto her chin. She scooped it up with her finger and licked it thoroughly.

The sight of her tongue so employed made Alex groan. His cock had begun to make its demands known so strenuously that he'd scarcely need the stimulation of the oysters. Still, he wasn't about to let that delicious tidbit go to waste. He scooped up a pastry from his own plate and put the entire thing into his mouth. The flaky pastry melted on his tongue, leaving him the savory oyster, with its hint of brine, to relish alone. Never had he enjoyed a meal more.

The next six courses continued to fan their ardor as either one or the other of them made lecherous comments or bold movements designed to inflame the other. By the time they reached the ice pudding, it was a miracle the delectable confection didn't melt from the heat they had generated between them. The dessert did not cool them off at all. When Emma used the tip of her tongue to taste the frozen treat, Alex could bear it no more.

Throwing his napkin down on his plate, he leaped to his feet, ran to her side of the table, and pulled her up into his arms.

She ran her tongue, still white from the pudding, around her lips. "Don't you want your dessert, Alex?"

"You are my dessert." His mouth descended onto hers, the sugariness of the ice pudding paling in comparison to that of her lips. Thrusting his tongue between them, he gloried in the tangle of sweet sensations, absolutely mad to have her here and now.

There was a huge expanse of table before them, but the logistics of her hooped skirts would prohibit that. Damned fashion. If only she was wearing a sleek, straight gown from the earlier part of the century, they might have had a chance to quench the flames that were licking his bones at this moment. However, there was the chair...

"Come here." He pulled Emma over to the chair where she'd enjoyed the sherry earlier. "If you will have a seat, my dear, I think we can have one final course before we leave."

"We can?" She frowned, but sat nevertheless. When he poked his head underneath her skirts, however, she gasped. "Alex!"

He ran his hands up her legs, over her lace-trimmed pantalettes until he came to her knees. With a gentle nudge, he parted them and continued to the apex of her thighs where the slit in her pantalettes gave him access to her warm womanly essence. Above him, her excited panting acted as a strong aphrodisiac. Emma had always responded to his slightest touch, but he'd not yet set a finger to her. Her excitement never failed to arouse him, and never more than now. His cock was straining at his breeches, eager to do its duty. Alex wasn't certain how that was going to be accomplished here at the Albion, but he'd certainly give his wife a release she'd never forget.

Parting the thin white fabric slowly, he inhaled her female musk, the delightful earthy scent of a woman. He leaned forward and placed his lips on her mons, a thrill shooting through him when she shuddered at his touch. When he touched his tongue to her intimate flesh, she writhed and moaned, shifting from side to side in the chair. Grinning, Alex licked deeper.

A sharp rap at the door brought him bolt upright, his head hitting the steel hoop canopied overtop of him.

Emma let out a shriek and clamped her legs shut.

Alex threw himself backward, trying in vain to escape from beneath the crinoline cage only to get caught in the myriad layers of silk and ruffles. "Just a minute," he called frantically. Good God, don't let anyone catch them in this lewd position. It would be the scandal of the Little Season.

Emma grabbed the edge of her skirt and jerked it up over his head, freeing him at last.

He glanced up at her, cheeks flushed, eyes wide, fear in every line of her face. "It's all right. I'll see who it is and get rid of them. It's likely only a waiter wanting to clear."

She nodded, then sat back in the chair, breathing hard.

Running a hand through his already tousled hair, Alex leaped to his feet, tugged his jacket into some semblance of order, then went to the door. Pulling himself up to his full height, he assumed a stern, displeased visage, and opened the door. "We are not—"

The words of dismissal died on his lips as he registered the form and florid face of Colonel Bray, the commanding officer for his regiment.

"Captain Bancroft. Well met, shhir." The slurred word gave Alex an idea of what the colonel had been doing this evening. "Thought I'd seen you come this way with yer wife. Pretty little thing. Can't miss that. Checked with th' waiter to make shhure, though, which room you're in."

"I'm honored that you would seek me out to say good evening, Colonel Bray." Alex hoped to God he wasn't as disheveled as he felt. He badly wanted to smooth down his hair once more, but didn't dare call attention to his scruffy appearance.

"N'tall, Captain. Wanted t' have a word with you as the t-t-topic of conversation at dinner happened to be about the upcoming deployment of the thhhhirtiethhhh." The colonel staggered toward him, the smell of port hanging heavily around his head.

"Indeed, sir." Alex peered at the man, bewildered. Why had Bray sought him out? He wasn't a familiar of the colonel at all. "Have we a date for departure for Canada now?"

"N' date yet, but I thought I ought to speak a word to you about the des...des...tination." Colonel Bray bent toward Alex's ear, as if about to impart a secret. "You need to keep this dry, Bancroft, but the regiment very well may be going in the opp...opposite direction."

Alex frowned, confused. What was the man talking about? "You don't mean we're going back to the Crimea, do you, sir?"

"I do not." The colonel straightened up, pointing a finger toward the ceiling, then grabbed Alex's shoulder and leaned in again. "Think farther east." He nodded and gave Alex a wink. "I've heard your bride's just returned from there."

Alex froze, appalled at what the man was suggesting.

"By the by, felicitations on your recent marriage, old chap." He patted Alex's shoulder. "Thought you'd like to know. I hope your lady wants to return to the Orient. Five years would be a long time to be without her."

"Is India assured, Colonel Bray?" Mind racing, Alex could only hope the colonel's low tones hadn't reached Emma's ears.

"Shhh! Not yet, not yet." Hay put his finger to his lips. "There's only talk at the moment, but those who're doin' the talkin' are the one's who'll do the decidin'."

That was what Alex was afraid of. "I see. Thank you, Colonel Bray, for giving me advance notice. I'll have to confer with my wife if the decision is made for India."

"Shhh, Bancroft. Keep it dry, Captain. Very dry." He laid his finger by his nose.

"I will, sir. You have my word on it." He'd take it to his grave if he lived that long. He could only hope the colonel would do so as well, despite his inebriated state. "Good evening, sir."

"G'd evenin', Bancroft." The older gentleman turned away, weaving and muttering as he left.

Alex stood at the door, not knowing what to think. Had Bray been so deep in his cups he'd misspoken about the regiment's change in postings? As much as he'd like to believe that, he doubted it. The topic would have to have been raised at the general's table for him to have had an inkling of the idea. It didn't seem likely he'd have made it up out of whole cloth. Even in his brandy befuddled haze, Bray had made the connection between Emma and India, suggesting the change had at least been discussed at his table. No, he had to assume the idea was, unfortunately, being considered.

Which made his most immediate dilemma whether or not to tell Emma.

If the rumor was only that—and Alex doubted their Canadian billet that had been talked of for months would be abandoned on a whim—then he really didn't need to mention it to his wife. Such gossip would only upset her terribly, and why should he do that when there was no real reason to believe it would ever come to pass? He'd check in at headquarters tomorrow and see if he could ascertain the truth. Whenever he knew something for certain would be plenty of time to inform Emma. Then together, they could plan for the sad but inevitable lengthy separation. And separation it must be. He'd no sooner ask his wife to return to the land that had terrorized her than he'd ask her to live on the moon.

"Who was that, Alex?"

He whipped around to find Emma standing directly behind him. How long had she been there? What had she heard?

Putting on a cheerful face, Alex took her arm and led her back into the room. "Colonel Bray wishing us felicitations on our marriage, my dear."

"How odd that he should choose to do it here."

"He was pretty well in his cups."

She nodded, then her brow puckered. "You look ill, dearest. Like you've seen a ghost or something. Are you certain that was all the colonel said to you?"

Alex opened his mouth, quite ready to lie to preserve his wife's peace of mind, but the sight of her sweet, worried eyes smote his heart. He could no more lie to her now than he could dishonor himself.

"Darling, come sit down." He led her over to the chair that was to have been the site of so much pleasure for them both. "Actually, the colonel did have some news for me. Let me pour you another sherry."

CHAPTER TWELVE

A MASS OF tangled needlework dangled from Emma's hands as she peered at the cheerful Ormolu clock on the mantlepiece for the tenth time this afternoon. Almost six o'clock. Finally, almost time for Alex to appear. Sighing, she righted the piece of cloth, took up her needle, and stabbed it into the sampler she couldn't quite keep her mind on. This time of night always put her nerves on edge. Waiting for her husband and word that the horrible rumor that he would be sent to India was true.

"Ouch." Once more, she'd not been attending and had stabbed her finger. She put the injured digit in her mouth to suck the bead of bright blood before it could leave another spot on her needlework. Although there were so many stains on it from similar injuries, she suspected it scarcely mattered anymore. Thus it had been for the past fortnight, ever since Alex and her lovely dinner had ended so dreadfully.

Downstairs the front door opened and closed.

Hastily, Emma set the needlework aside, then sat up straighter in her chair, hands clasped neatly in her lap. Staring straight at the door Alex was about to come through, she squeezed her fingers, the pain of the motion distracting her from thoughts of how she would ever cope if Alex entered and announced he was sailing to India.

Heavy footfalls sounded on the stairs. Hardly the joyous steps of a man with good news to tell. Emma gritted her teeth and prepared her false smile.

The door opened, admitting Alex, whose mouth was set in a thin, straight line.

Her heart stuttered. He'd never looked so grim on any of the previous nights when he'd arrived with no news. She sucked in her breath and steeled herself as best she could. "So it *is* India then?"

Alex's miserable eyes met hers and he nodded. "I've had confirmation today from Colonel Bray." His shoulders sagged. "We leave mid-December."

The breath Emma had been holding unawares rushed out, leaving her empty. Her heart fluttered and she fought not to swoon, although sinking down into oblivion would be a blessing at the moment. Five years without Alex. Five long years without his touch, without his arms around her to keep her safe. It was inconceivable. Impossible to endure. She dropped her head in her hands as the burning tears began to flow.

Then his arms were around her, the embrace that made her feel so safe and loved. And would soon be no more than a memory. She buried her face in his chest and sobbed into the scarlet tunic that she loved because it meant safety. No more.

"Emma. Emma. Please don't cry." He hugged her to him. "We have to be brave about this, don't you see?"

"No, no, I don't see, Alex." She shook her head, his wool uniform scratchy against her face. She raised it to him, imploring. "It's not fair for the army to take you away from me for five long years. We've not been married three months yet and now, before we can even spend one Christmas together, you'll be leaving for an eternity." Her sobs continued and she didn't try to stop them. "I'll be all alone."

He held her closer, rubbing her back and crooning to her. "Hush, my love. You won't be alone, I promise. I'll arrange for you to stay with Uncle Jack and Aunt Lucinda. So you won't be alone. Not at all."

"I *will* be alone, Alex." She reared back, anger sharpening her words. "Because you won't be here with me."

"Then what would you have me do, my dear?" His jaw tightened and his brow puckered. "Resign my commission?"

Staring straight into his eyes, Emma uttered a single word. "Yes."

He stared back at her, uncomprehending. "What do you mean, 'yes?' I cannot resign my commission. I owe my duty to queen and country."

"You also owe a duty to wife and family, don't you, Alex?" Her determined stare never wavered. "Of course, if you leave for five years, we won't be having a family." That would be bad enough, but the alternative was worse. "Or if I get with child before you sail, you may never know that you are a father. Never see your child or be with me when it is born. How can you agree to miss the most important moments of our life together?"

As if her words had barbs, he flinched and hung his head. "I cannot resign my commission, Emma. What would I do? How would I provide for you and our children? I've been in the army since I was eighteen. I know no other kind of employment fit for a gentleman."

"You don't need employment." She took him by the shoulders, impatient to make him understand. "Didn't you tell me that you'll be given an estate and ten thousand pounds for marrying me? We can certainly live on such a sum, especially with the income an estate will generate."

Alex sighed, his lips settling into a thin line. "That is not yet assured, Emma. It depends on whether or not my cousins keep their part of the wager and marry by August. Until that time, nothing is for certain."

"We can access funds from my dowry then. It's substantial, as you know. My uncle's shares in the East India Company alone would provide for us amply for the rest of our lives. We could buy an estate in the country or a townhouse here in London and live happily-ever-after with our sons and daughters around us."

Staring straight into his eyes, she earnestly tried to see into his soul. "And no one would need to go to India or anywhere else."

His face grew stern, his eyes shuttered. A small tic at the left corner of his mouth twitched intermittently. It did so whenever Alex was under a great deal of stress, she'd noticed. "I will not be a man who lives off his wife's money, Emma. Those funds are for you and our children if something happens to me. I hope you know me well enough to realize I will not touch that money."

"I hope I know you well enough to believe you are not a man who abandons his wife and children for an army that doesn't give a damn about you." Swearing wasn't ladylike, but by God, she'd fight like a man to keep her husband with her. "If it did, you'd have been promoted to major by now."

"That's not true, Emma." Alex's face had gone white. Now it flushed red. "In fact, Colonel Bray has informed me that with this new posting, I'll be advanced to the rank of major, effective immediately upon our arrival in Calcutta."

How cruel the army was. Alex had hoped the new billet in Canada would bring about his long-sought promotion to major. By rights, he should have already been raised to that rank, but it simply had not happened. Now the only way to get the promotion, his dream for so long, was to tear him from her and send him far away for years upon years. Unless she...

Emma jerked away from him as if her hands had been burned. "I cannot return to India, Alex. You know that. You know why."

"I do." He nodded his head furiously. "I would never ask that of you, my dear." Cautiously, he slid his finger down her cheek. "But neither should you ask me to resign. I cannot do so, and you also know why."

"What if you transferred to another regiment?" Grasping at straws, she fought to think of anything that might keep him here with her.

"I could do so, but the advancement to major would not be assured. At least, not for a number of years."

The sadness in his voice wrenched her heart, but there seemed to be no remedy for their heartbreak. "Then we are both bound to a pain-filled span of years, my dear. And, I suspect, when you return, our life can never be what it was or might have been. We will have missed the most precious years of our life together." Emma gazed at his face, a mirror of her misery, and tears began to trickle down her cheeks once more. "I only hope you can learn to live with that."

NEXT EVENING, EMMA sat in their bedchamber, dressed in her sheerest nightgown of white Indian muslin, the design of which just happened to accentuate her bosom more than any other garment she owned. She'd applied her favorite perfume and touched her cheeks with rouge from the pot she kept hidden in her trunk. Her heavy ruby earrings swung seductively from her ears, catching the candlelight and hopefully the eye of one Captain Alex Bancroft.

After their argument last evening and the ensuing night spent apart, Emma had wracked her brain for a means to persuade her husband that they would both be better off if he remained at home in England with her. In the wee hours of the morning, she'd hit upon what she hoped would be the perfect method of persuasion.

She'd sent a note to Alex that they would be dining in the bedchamber that evening. What she hadn't told him was that the feasting would begin somewhere other than the dining table that had been set before the fireplace. She hoped her husband had eaten heartily at lunch, as they would likely not enjoy their dinner until well after midnight.

The entry doorknob rattled.

One of the best things about their bedchamber was its location directly above the foyer. The slam of the front door was easily heard here, warning Emma of the approach of her husband. Immediately, she sat straighter, bowing her back slightly so her breasts jutted out beneath the delicate fabric. She believed, if Alex looked close enough, he'd be able to see the dark circles of her nipples.

As the door opened, Emma smiled her brightest.

Alex entered, his brow furrowed. "Your note said you wished to eat in our chamber. Nothing is amiss, is it, Emma?"

He was worried about her. That was good.

"Not in the least, my dear." She rose and started toward him, swaying her hips with each step. "I thought that a leisurely, intimate evening might be called for, is all. We've been so worried about the news from your regiment, and now that it has come, perhaps the best thing for us to do is spend the evening simply." She licked her lips. "Enjoying one another's…company."

"But you seem ready for bed, my dear." He eyed her gown. "Are you certain you are not fatigued?"

"Oh no, my love." She started on the buttons of his tunic. "Quite the contrary. I only wanted to be as comfortable as possible." His garment now stood open, revealing his undershirt, the muscles of his chest stretching the fabric. "You should too."

"Indeed." He peered down at her as she pulled his tunic off.

"Yes, so I've ordered a bath for you before dinner." She busied herself with laying his uniform on the bed and taking up his dressing gown that she'd laid out, a silky dark blue garment he usually wore. "James has set the tub in the dressing room. It should be filled by now." She helped him slip the robe on, then took her time tying the sash.

"You are being very wifely this evening, my dear." Alex followed her every move as she pulled the bow tight.

"If we only have a few weeks before you must leave, we shouldn't spend them being cross with one another, should we?" Emma ran her hand up the lapel of the dressing gown, his chest warm and hard beneath it.

"Absolutely not." He grabbed her up and seized her lips,

thrusting his tongue between them, ravishing her mouth with an air of desperation.

So very good. Their lack of intimate relations last evening would play into her plan nicely. With an effort, she broke the kiss and backed away. "Bath first, please."

He groaned but hurried dutifully to the dressing room. The gleaming copper washtub fit snugly in the room with just enough room to maneuver around it. Emma followed him in and shut the door. "Do you need assistance with the rest of your clothing? Shall I call Phillips?"

Alex sent her a lecherous grin. "I think my valet can be dispensed with if you will lend me a hand."

"My pleasure." She managed to give the word every ounce of sensuality she could before grasping his waistband and unbuttoning his trousers. Once done, she snaked the garment down over his hips, his shirt falling over the evidence of his growing interest. "Sit there," she indicated a chair in the corner, "and take off your boots. I'll step out while you step into the tub."

He snared her hand to halt her as she tried to leave. "You'll return to wash my back, won't you, sweetheart?"

"You can depend upon it, my love." Swiftly, she left him, excitement building within her. She would win her husband back from the allure of the army no matter what it took.

When she returned, Alex sat naked in the water, his curly dark head leaning back against the rim of the metal tub, eyes closed, looking more peaceful than she'd seen him in weeks. "You look very comfortable."

"Ummm, I am comfortable. The water is perfectly warm." He opened his eyes to gaze at her longingly. "Thank you for arranging this, especially after last night. You know I'd stay here with you if I could, Emma."

"I know." Emma knelt beside the tub, careful to let the neck of her gown fall open, exposing her breasts to Alex's avid gaze. His low moan confirmed that he'd seen them. "Shall I wash your back now?"

She leaned across the tub to grab the soap, allowing the front of her gown to fall into the water. When she pulled back, the thin material clung tightly to her body, showing every rounded contour of her bosom. Even better, as the fabric cooled, her nipples hardened, the stiff little points jutting out in all their glory.

"You seem to have gotten wet, my dear." His gaze fastened on her breasts as his breath quickened. Something stirred down under the water.

"I did, didn't I?" Emma made as if to pull herself up from the floor, but as she did, she leaned over the tub, making sure the rest of the front of her gown dipped into the water. When she stepped back, the gown clung to her body like a second skin, delineating every curve. "Oh, dear, I seem to have made it worse."

Then, to make certain of the effect, she reached to the back of her gown and pulled the cloth tight against her skin, accentuating the dark triangle at the top of her thighs, clearly visible through the wet garment.

Her husband's eyes grew round and darkened to jet black in an instant. He grabbed her hand and pulled her to him. Frantically, his mouth sought her nipple, then with a growl, he engulfed it.

The sensation of his tongue rubbing the cloth across her sensitive flesh set her core to throbbing. She threw her head back, pressing her breast harder into his mouth. "That feels so incredibly good, Alex."

With no other warning than a low growl, he pulled her into the tub. Water splashed everywhere, soaking her entirely, but Emma cared not at all. Her plan was working magnificently. If only she could keep her mind focused—a much harder chore than she'd believed when all she wanted to do was give in to the delicious sensations.

Slowly, she maneuvered her legs into the tub until they lay inside with her knees bent on either side of Alex's, his member rising straight up between them. She straightened and, with one hand, pulled the dripping gown up and over her head, letting it fall with a wet *plop* onto the floor.

Carefully, she rose up overtop of him and, as his jaw dropped, slid herself down inch by inch over his rampant cock until she was fully impaled on him. Smiling, she leaned forward and took his head in both her hands. "How does that feel?"

In answer, he seized her face, pulled her to him, and plunged his tongue into her mouth.

Immediately, his member surged upward inside her, filling her more completely than she'd ever thought possible. Her throbbing core became an insistent beat as she began to rise and fall, riding him like a stallion she was trying to break. Only she didn't want to break this stallion—far from it. She wanted to ride him into a frenzy until they dissolved into one another and became one.

Alex growled again and again as he thrust into her, still holding the kiss, her tongue a willing prisoner. Their frantic pumping sent a spray of water all over the chamber, but neither one cared. Emma continued to ride him, clenching her hot sheath around him until the intensity of his thrusts increased, bringing her throbbing core to the ultimate release. She shrieked his name as her pleasure burst upon her. No sooner had she done so when Alex shouted hoarsely and she was filled with liquid heat as he spent himself entirely.

Slowly, Emma lowered herself into the cooling water until she lay panting on Alex's heaving chest. His heart hammered in her ear, a sweet cadence as she lay pillowed on top of him. How could she ever let this man go?

He wrapped his arms around her, that feeling of comfort and safety stealing through her as always. "You do realize you almost killed me just then." His deep voice rumbled through his chest. "It was a very close thing."

"I think you'll take some killing yet." She grinned against his chest.

"I'm not so sure about that."

"You wait and see."

When they finally caught their breath, Emma rose on wobbly

legs, wrapped herself in a large towel, and strode toward the bedroom. She paused at the threshold to look over her shoulder at her husband, still laid back in the bathtub, and asked, "Are you coming?"

The loud groan that followed her out of the dressing room was everything she could have hoped for. She continued to their tall bed, dropped her towel then crawled up onto the turned-back sheets. Lying down on her side facing the dressing room, she propped her head up on her hand. And waited.

After some minutes, which seemed an hour at least, Alex emerged, towel around his midsection. He stopped at the sight of her in the bed.

With deliberation, she raised one leg so her foot remained flat on the mattress while the other leg stayed straight. A clearer invitation to join her she could not have imagined.

The towel fluttered to the floor as Alex strode the few steps then launched onto the bed. He landed next to her, then pushed her onto her back, covered her, and buried his face between her breasts.

Reveling in the weight of his body on top of hers, always so arousing, Emma had to make herself focus on the task at hand. She had more in mind for her husband now. "Alex?"

"Hmmm." He continued kissing and caressing her breasts, a most pleasant distraction, but she was determined to stick to her course.

"Can you sit up for a moment?"

Very reluctantly, he did so, though his fingers still stroked her nipple.

Emma took a breath, thought about exactly what she wanted to do, then pulled her legs up, knees bent. "Can you sit between my legs?"

"Of course, my love." Smiling lasciviously, he moved to his knees then sat staring at her body, so completely opened to him. "Did you perhaps wish to continue where we left off at the Albion?"

Tempting as that was, it wasn't her plan for tonight. "Not exactly." She slid her left leg out and a little to the side. "Come closer."

Wary now, he inched toward her, his cock stirring with interest. "Like this?" He brushed it against her opening and a pleasurable throb began deep inside her.

Her husband had only to touch her and she was ready for him. "Yes, exactly like that." With a little effort, she lifted her right leg until her ankle rested on his broad shoulder. "Now enter me."

Eyes dark as jet, Alex leaned forward then thrust inside her. Deep inside her. The intensity of his stare as he started to move within her made this the most intimate thing she'd ever experienced. Like they were actually becoming one with each other.

The rhythm he set was slow, but it built in minute increments until Emma wanted to explode from within. "Oh, Alex," she moaned, at last unable to keep silent. "I didn't realize how good this would feel." She throbbed and ached each time he thrust into her. And all she wanted was more. Gazing into his face, she was alarmed to see his jaw clenched and sweat popping out on his forehead. "Are you all right?"

"Holding back," he ground out. "Waiting for your pleasure." He thrust even deeper and Emma gasped as her body wound itself tighter within. "Don't hold back." She panted as he immediately sped up. "Let go now."

With a loud cry, Alex plunged into her deeply, then thrust sharply several times. Emma arched her back and shrieked as she shattered around him, the pleasure more intense than ever before. Her cry was joined by Alex bellowing her name. Her toes curled as he gave a final thrust and spent himself, straining against her for what seemed an age.

Both sated, Alex gently lowered her leg, then collapsed onto the bed.

Emma lay back panting and staring up at the blue brocade canopy, lost in a love-induced haze. Never had she experienced such a joining with her husband. Nor been so exhausted by their lovemaking. She closed her eyes, about to drift off to sleep, when Alex's voice came to her as from a long way off.

"Emma?"

"Hmmm?"

"What did you do?"

"What?" She was too sleepy to talk.

"How did you know what to do just then? Putting your leg up like that?" His voice was hushed, yet his tone was…suspicious.

Wide awake now, Emma rolled over to find him watching her intently.

"I know you were a virgin when we married. There was blood on the sheets." His gaze never wavered from her face. "However, what we just did…I've never felt such a powerful release in my life. How did you know how to do that?"

Emma smiled and stroked his cheek. "Remember I told you all of my memories of India weren't bad?"

He nodded, still wary.

"Well, when my uncle and aunt and I first arrived in India, we traveled for something like a week to visit Wajid Ali Shah, the then ruler of Oudh. Uncle Washer had been sent by the East India Company to tour India and check up on their business interests, I suppose. I was fourteen at the time, so I didn't pay much attention to those conversations. But we were in Oudh for a month or more, going each day to the palace for my uncle to meet with the king. While the men talked and ate, my aunt and I were welcomed into the *zenana*, the part of the palace where all the women lived, including Wajid Shah's wives."

Emma propped her head up on her hand and glanced away, unsure how her husband would take some parts of this tale. Still, she needed to tell him to keep him from mistrusting her. "My aunt spoke each day with the older women and wives, but I found a young girl my exact same age, and we became good friends."

"But how did you understand one another? You hadn't

learned Hindi, had you?" At least Alex seemed interested in the story. That would be helpful.

"No, although I eventually picked up a smattering of the language as we traveled around the country. But no, at that time, I knew nothing of Hindi. The girl, whose name was Lakshmi, had learned some English from missionaries who had visited the *zenana*. And she taught me my first words and phrases in Hindi, so we managed to speak quite well after a time."

"What does Lakshmi have to do with your...knowledge of what we just did?" That suspicious tone was back in Alex's voice.

"Because she was the newest of Wajid Shah's wives."

"What?" Alex shot up in the bed. "At fourteen?"

"Yes, fourteen is a perfectly acceptable age for marriage in India." Emma bit back a smile and patted the bed. "Lay back down, please. I'd have thought the idea of multiple wives would have given you more concern."

"Well, but I've known about that for ages." Alex settled back into the mattress. "But to marry at fourteen?"

"Have you forgotten your history lessons? Queen Katherine Howard, one of Henry VIII's wives, married him when she was fifteen." Emma stroked Alex's cheek. "Here in England, we marry at eighteen without a qualm, sometimes seventeen."

"Well, fourteen and eighteen or even seventeen are vastly different." Her husband did not seem inclined to let this go.

"Despite your objections, Lakshmi was indeed married to the Shah, and I'm sure her parents were thrilled for her to marry a king. She herself was all starry-eyed at the time because she had, as she put it, 'found favor with her husband.' I wasn't quite sure what that meant until the last day before we were to leave when she told me." Emma recalled being quite shocked, but also very interested in what Lakshmi had explained to her.

"So this girl told you how to..." Alex winced, as though he might have to avoid a blow.

"She called it 'splitting the bamboo.'" Emma giggled. She'd thought it funny when Lakshmi told her about it. "She is the one who told me about what goes on in the marriage bed."

"How were you allowed to know such things, Emma?" Alex whispered, as if someone might hear him. "Proper young ladies are sheltered from anything having to do with marital congress until after they are married."

"My aunt was absorbed with the older women. She never knew anything about it." Thank goodness. Aunt Washer would have surely had a conniption. "The Indian women in the *zenana* may or may not have known. If they did, they would have thought she was doing me a favor." Emma had doubted they knew at the time. They hadn't seemed interested in her at all. And Lakshmi was a wife and considered a woman. What she told the English girl was no concern of theirs.

"So why did you think of this, splitting the bamboo today, love?" His voice had become softer, cajoling.

"Because I wanted to 'find favor' with my husband." She ran her hand down his naked side, making him shiver. "Did I find favor with you, my love?"

He pulled her to him and crushed her to his chest. "You have always found favor with me, my darling. Never, ever doubt that."

Emma gloried in his embrace, then gently pulled herself away. "I also did it to make you realize all the things I can do for you—and to you—that the army can never do."

He stiffened and shot a hurt look at her through narrowed eyes.

"Are you willing to give up all this joy, all our passion, when you need not?" Emma sat up, pulling the covers up over her. "If you resign your commission, I have no doubt that, with your skills and intelligence, you can find other employment that will be just as satisfying as serving queen and country. You have friends and relations who would be eager to help you in any way they can. Won't you consider asking them to help us?"

Alex fell back on the bed, arm flung over his face. "You must give me some time, Emma. This is not a decision I can make lightly."

"I understand, my dear. You are torn between two duties. One to the only life you've ever known, the other to your life yet to come." Emma spoke softly. Her husband could not be driven to make this choice. He needed to come to it on his own. "I shall be disappointed if you choose to stay your present course, but I will love you no matter what decision you reach."

Emma lay back on the bed, pulling the covers up to her chin against the sudden chill in the room. She'd done her best to make Alex see his choices clearly, to realize his life with her would be the better course for both of them. Now all she could do was pray he made the best decision for them both.

Chapter Thirteen

A WEEK AFTER being thoroughly seduced by his wife, Alex strolled into Langham's looking for his Uncle Jack. Still unsure of the decision he needed to make, and with time running out rapidly—today was the sixteenth of November and the regiment's sail date had been set as December the twelfth—Alex had finally decided he needed another, non-military opinion and would seek out his uncle. During the past week, he'd spoken with several of the married officers, including Mac, who was in the throes of packing up his household.

"Go to India by all means, Bancroft." His friend stretched out in a chair at headquarters, looking as pleased as a cat with cream on its whiskers. "That's your ticket to the rise in rank, isn't it? If your wife declines to go, what can you do? You don't want to force her," he winked, "not when I hear there are all manner of ladies in the Orient with whom you can dip your wick."

Mac got a dreamy look on his face. "Exotic women who…know things."

Alex had turned away, afraid his face would betray the fact his wife knew things as well. He needn't sail halfway around the world to find adventure in another woman's arms. Not when he had Emma in his bed right here. What he needed badly was someone to help him rationalize the monumental decision to resign his commission. He wouldn't find that at headquarters.

Unfortunately, both positions had merits and drawbacks. But which one would lead to his ultimate happiness? That was why he wanted to consult his uncle.

A roar went up, bringing Alex back to the present. Uncle Jack was currently engaged in a match with a much younger opponent, but despite the difference in both age and size, his uncle was giving the man a drubbing. The crowd had responded to a crisp uppercut Jack had given his adversary and Alex rubbed his chin in sympathy. He'd been in that chap's boots before.

"Alex."

He turned to find his cousin Julius standing to the side, his little black book in hand. With a grin spreading over his face, Alex strode over to him. "Julius, well met. Are you here to box?"

"Never in this lifetime." His cousin looked appalled. "I'm here to put wagers on your uncle from Francis, Yule, and Tom. The others couldn't be reached." Julius raised a brow. "Are you boxing with him today?"

"God forbid, Jules. The man's a powerhouse. Pounds me to dust every time I face him in the ring. No, I just need to speak to him about a personal matter." Alex hesitated. Julius, while he might be part of Grandfather's wager, wouldn't have reason to steer him wrong if he asked his opinion. "I could use your advice as well, cousin."

Julius put away his book and pencil and faced Alex. "You now have my attention."

"My regiment is shipping out to India on the twelfth of next month. My wife cannot go back there for personal reasons you don't need to know. But trust me, they are valid. This means we will be parted for five very long years. The silver lining is I'll be given a promotion to major that's been a long time coming, with its attendant increase in pay. The only alternative I have would be to resign my commission, stay in England, and seek new employment, for which I have not trained."

Fixing him with a stern eye, Julius shook his head. "So you have to choose between the army or your wife." He scoffed disgustedly. "Choose your wife, Alex. For God's sake, it shouldn't have been a choice at all. You can't leave her, you just married the woman. Employment can be had anywhere. Hell, you can come be my land agent. I need to fire my current one. He's half up the pole most days. Who knows what he's missing in his alcoholic fog?"

"I haven't the first idea about estate management, Jules." Alex shook his head. "Isn't there something else a gentleman can do?"

"Do you have a taste for either the law or medicine? I daresay the Church is out."

"You'd say correctly. None of those professions sound remotely like anything I would wish to do for the rest of my life. I'd do better to hold prize fights and wager on them for a living." He motioned to his uncle, who'd just sent his opponent to the ring's floor.

Uncle Jack offered the man a hand, helped him up, then strode over to the corner where Alex and Julius stood. He leaned over the rope. "What did I hear you say? There's to be a wager?"

When Alex had finally apprised his uncle of what was actually going on, the older man shook his head and made a sound of disgust. "Come up into this ring this minute so I can knock some sense into you, nephew."

Alex winced. His uncle's bellow could be heard throughout the room.

"Of course you cannot go off and leave poor Emma for five years. Have you truly taken leave of your senses?" Uncle Jack climbed through the ropes to stand beside him.

"No, uncle. I don't wish to leave Emma, but the army is my profession. What else am I to do if I resign my commission? Once the commission fee is spent, how will we live?"

"Well, there's Grandfather's wager," Julius broke in. "After next August, you could be set for life with money and an estate."

"Only if everyone else does their part. To date it's only me and maybe Sandy." Alex nodded to his cousin. "Have we heard what happened with him?"

"I haven't." Julius shrugged. "The whole thing was rather bizarre, but I'm hoping for the best."

Alex closed his eyes. The family wager wasn't turning out as much of a certainty as he'd hoped. "So you see, uncle, there's nothing assured about my future if I resign."

"If that's the only obstacle, I'll be happy to deed one of my small estates over to you. There's one in Shropshire with about a thousand acres, and a few tenant farms for income." His uncle wiped his brow on his towel. "It's unentailed, so I may do with it what I wish. Let me give it to you, nephew, as a belated wedding present. Then you may put your poor wife's mind at ease."

The offer was both generous and tempting. He and Emma could live comfortably in the country on his commission fee once it was returned to him. Between that and Emma's fortune and the income from the farms, they could have a wonderful life together. However, it wouldn't be money earned from his own labors. If he inherited property, or won it as he might from Grandfather if the marriage wager was eventually completed, that would be different. But a gift, after his uncle had already been so generous, didn't set well with him. He'd be giving up his profession, giving up his promotion. By God, he wouldn't give up his pride as well.

"I thank you for that most generous offer, uncle. But I must decline it."

"What?" Uncle Jack's head snapped around so quickly his neck cracked.

"What?" Julius stepped back he was so startled.

"Neither of you is looking at this from my perspective. What kind of husband would I be if I couldn't provide for my wife and children on my own?" He raised his hands to still their objections. "Don't worry. I'll transfer to another regiment so I can remain with Emma, then all I've lost is my chance at the promotion. Maybe in five years or so, there'll be another opportunity. I just hope Colonel Bray won't take offense. He wants me to go to India very badly." Alex clenched his jaw. Everything seemed set against him. "He could make the transfer extremely difficult."

"What about a wager?" Uncle Jack thumped him on the chest.

"A wager about what? Whether or not I can transfer to another regiment?" His uncle wasn't making sense. Of course, gentlemen wagered on everything, but this seemed frivolous at best considering the circumstances.

"No, on a boxing match between the two of us." Uncle Jack nodded to Julius, who pulled out his book and pencil.

"Why, uncle?" Perhaps his last bout had jiggled the man's brains.

"So that you will accept my offer and settle down with Emma. She deserves to not be dragged from one post to another for the next twenty or so years." Uncle Jack crossed his arms over his chest. "And you will have a new profession as a landowner where you will be your own man, rather than having your superiors tell you what to do."

"Then what is the wager?" Not that he wished to leave the army, but he'd hear his uncle out.

"If you win, you get the property in Shropshire free and clear and become a landed gentleman."

"And if I lose?"

"Then you will give me half of Emma's fortune…"

Alex's brows shot up. That was a substantial amount of money. And Emma's money to boot. Not something to take lightly.

"And you will transfer to the AGS." Uncle Jack stared at him, unwavering.

"What's the AGS?" That seemed like an odd stipulation. He didn't think his uncle was overly familiar with the army's regiments.

"The Army Gymnastic Staff, a new corps created by an old friend of mine, Colonel Fredric Hamilton. Their sole purpose is to train the troops in gymnastics for their physical fitness. Currently, they focus on teaching fencing and gymnastics, but I'm trying to persuade Hamilton to include boxing." His uncle looked positively gleeful. "With you on staff, I might just get my way."

Mind whirling, Alex tried to remember all his options. He could take his uncle's generous offer of the estate in Shropshire and be done with it. The easiest solution by far. To do so, however, he knew would stick in his craw forever. He wasn't one to take charity, no matter how kindly meant.

He could resign his commission and try to find employment elsewhere. A solution fraught with peril as his skills were limited. The simplest solution would be to transfer to another regiment, which although easy enough, had begun to pall on him. If he couldn't remain with the 30th—and he understood well that he could not—or have the promotion he deserved, he'd begun to think he didn't wish to remain in the army at all.

And then there was his uncle's outlandish wager.

Certainly, Uncle Jack was counting on the fact that Alex couldn't resist a wager. Undeniably true, because if he would wager he could meet and marry a woman in less than a fortnight, he'd take any wager that came along. Exactly why Alex was now considering his uncle's proposal very, very seriously.

Pitted against his uncle, this match would scarcely be a fair fight unless he set himself to training immediately, which he could do right here at Langham's. And considering the side wagering he could do with his cousins and grandfather, he could come out very wealthy indeed if he won. It was, in a word, irresistible.

Alex stuck out his hand and his uncle took it. "Done."

In the background, Julius was scratching the pencil frantically in his book, muttering. "Francis, Harry, Tom, Yule. Sandy's in Scotland, I'll have to send for him. And Grandfather. Good. The notes will go out tonight informing them of the match." Jules looked at Uncle Jack. "When do you intend to fight? It's going to take a little time to get everyone gathered here for the match. No one's going to want to miss this."

His uncle looked Alex up and down. "If you want to win, you're going to have to train. Two weeks should give you a fighting chance." He glanced at Julius. "Will that be enough time for you?"

"Ample." His cousin grinned at Alex. "I'll have everyone here in Town before December first. I expect the wagering will be fierce." He chuckled. "But I can't tell you if they'll wager for you or against you."

AFTER WAITING ALL day to hear from Alex, Emma had ordered a bath to be drawn for her in the dressing room. She hoped to soothe her nerves, ready to crack with tension waiting for him to make his decision. Surely, she couldn't sustain this façade of calm much longer. In desperation, she'd even entertained the idea of accompanying him to India, but only for the briefest minutes. Even so, her body had trembled for a quarter of an hour afterwards. No, she couldn't do that if her life depended on it.

So her husband would have to make his decision. She could only pray he would choose to stay with her.

Emma eased down into the steaming water, tendrils of her hair escaping from the tortoise shell combs with which Cooper had secured the tresses on top of her head. Stretching out in the tub, she slid down until her body was completely submerged save for her head, and let her body relax. The scent of lavender oil she'd poured into the water helped keep her tranquil. This was so peaceful she could drift right off here…

The door opening brought Emma back up to consciousness, though her eyes remained closed. "I'm not quite ready to emerge yet, Cooper. Can you pour some hot water in, please?"

Water began to trickle in, warming her toes.

"Thank you, Cooper. Please inform me when Captain Bancroft arrives."

Something hovered near her head.

"I have arrived, sweetheart," he whispered in her ear.

With a scream, Emma bolted up out of the water, twisting around to face her smiling husband.

The smile turned into a grin as he took in her shiny, wet, naked body. "You have to give me this kind of welcome every day from now on, my love. I can't think of anything else that would be a better greeting."

"Alex, you wretch." She tried her best to shield her body with her hands, but there was too much of her and too few hands. Besides, he'd done more than look at her last night. Much more. She straightened and held out a hand. "Please hand me a towel."

"Are you certain you're done with your bath? Don't you want me to scrub your back?" Laughing, he held the towel just out of her reach.

"Wretched man." Emma rose from the tub, all peace and serenity fled. "The towel, Captain Bancroft."

"Don't you want to know why I'm home so early?" Dangling the towel over her head, Alex coaxed her closer to him.

She glanced into the bedchamber, still bright with daylight. "You are early. Why?" She jumped up, making a grab for the towel, her breasts bouncing freely."

"Because I'm in training."

Emma stopped, heart in her throat. "For India?" All the strength ran out of her legs and she sat down on the chair that had held the towel. "You're leaving me then?"

"No, darling, no." Alex rushed to her and gathered her into his arms. "No, I'm handing in my resignation tomorrow. In two weeks, when everyone else is leaving for Calcutta, hopefully we will be setting up house. Together."

"Oh, Alex!" She threw her arms around him, hugging him until her body ached with the scratchy wool of his tunic. "You chose me."

"Of course I did, darling." He lifted her chin and kissed her lips. "I only needed time to find the pathway through the tangle. Now I'll be able to provide for us and our family when we have one. Today, I found that way through, thanks to Uncle Jack."

"Uncle Jack? How odd. What did he do?" She rested her head on his shoulder.

"He's challenged me to a wager on a boxing match with him in two weeks' time. If I win, he gives us an estate with tenant farms to manage as I see fit so we can live quite comfortably as landed gentry." He kissed her head and nuzzled her ear.

"And if you lose?" That was the more important question, but as he intended to stay in England, it was almost a moot point. They would be together; that was all that mattered to her.

Alex hesitated, and her heart leapt into her throat. "Uncle Jack wins half your dowry."

Good lord. That quite knocked the breath out of her.

"And I end up in some newfangled army corps that's training soldiers in physical fitness." He grimaced. "In Aldershot, of all places." Alex looked at her sheepishly. "I know it's a lot to ask, wagering your money, but I thought—"

"So no matter what happens with the wager, you're not leaving for India?" She wanted to make absolutely certain that was correct. The money was a serious concern, but it had come from her uncle and the East India Company. If it could take away the possibility of Alex going to India, it was worth every penny.

"No, sweetheart. I hand in the papers tomorrow. I think if I tried to leave you, my entire family would grind me to a pulp." He smiled ruefully.

"Alex, oh, Alex!" Emma threw herself into his arms, happier now than on her wedding day. "Thank you, thank you."

"You can best thank me," he whispered in her ear, "by remembering some more positions from your friend the Indian Princess." Then he clamped his hand onto her mound, his fingers seeking entry to her wet, warm sheath.

Overwhelming happiness made her widen her stance, giving him easy access to her. His thumb brushed her mons, making her shudder, then he slid it down toward her opening and...stopped.

Straining toward him, so tantalizingly near to feeling him inside her, Emma hitched her leg up over his hip and thrust toward him. To her utter amazement, he backed away, a look of disgust on his face.

"Alex, what's wrong?"

With a deep sigh, he shook his head. "I can't. I promised Julius I wouldn't…we wouldn't be intimate until after the match with Uncle Jack."

"Why not?" She almost screamed at him. They had every reason to celebrate tonight. And he was going to say no?

"Abstinence makes you fight better. All serious fighters abstain for several weeks before big fights."

"You've never done that before when you were fighting with your uncle." She reached out to him, and he stepped backward so quickly he almost stumbled. He really could not be serious about this, could he?

"I've never had so much riding on a fight before. The last time Uncle Jack beat me so badly, do you remember the night before the match? You had leaned over the bed wearing only your crinoline and pantalettes and I came up behind you and—"

"Yes, I remember that exceedingly well, thank you." If he wasn't going to take care of her needs, she certainly didn't want to remember a time when he had done so—spectacularly. "So you're not going to touch me for two weeks?"

He shrugged. "Two weeks of restraint for a home of our own is a small price to pay."

This would be unbearable, did he not understand that? "When and where is this fight being held? If I can't have intimate pleasures with my husband for a fortnight *and* must have my future decided by fisticuffs of all things, then I'm going to be there."

Alex looked stricken. "But, sweetheart, you *can't* go there. Women aren't allowed in the boxing area. House rules. You cannot attend." He reached out to her then snatched his hand back. "I'll send you word the moment the match is over."

Winding the towel around her at last, Emma nodded. House rules be damned. She would see about breaking those rules, no matter what the house said.

"I MUST TELL you, my dear, I have never been so relieved in all my life." Stirring her tea, Emma watched as the milk swirled around the cup, turning the dark brown brew a pleasant shade of tan. "Well, almost the most relieved." She sipped the tea and sighed with contentment. "Uncle Jack is so very generous, Lucinda. We cannot thank you both enough."

Lucinda took a sip from her cup, made a pinched face, then added two more lumps of sugar to the two already in there. "Jack should have given that estate to Alex outright."

"Apparently, he tried to do just that, but my stubborn husband wouldn't take it. He said he wanted to earn it on his own with this wager." Emma sighed deeply. "I suppose he believes a wager can solve any problem."

"Well, I can tell you I do not. This boxing wager is going to upset my nerves terribly." She gave Emma a sly look. "I suppose Alex is in training these next two weeks as well?"

"Yes, more's the pity." His ultimatum about abstinence in the marriage bed was going to upset more than her nerves. "I was more than a little piqued last evening when Alex removed himself to the guest bedroom, 'for the duration' he said."

"Jack has done the same thing." Lucinda sounded aggrieved. "I've a good mind to begin a campaign to make him break that vow." She glanced at Emma and blushed. "You must think me the most indelicate woman alive, Emma."

"Not at all, my dear." Emma patted her hand. "I'd do the same thing if so much weren't riding on this silly match. I can't imagine how lonely my nights will be until it's over." Best not to think about that. Last night had been such a trial, alone in their big bed. She took up a cucumber and dill sandwich and chewed thoughtfully. "To make it worse, Alex won't even entertain the idea of me attending the match. With so much riding on it, I think I should be entitled to witness it, don't you?"

"I do, but Jack has told me the same thing. Has forbidden me, in fact, to even mention attending the match because of my 'interesting condition." She glanced down at her torso, now almost seven months along with child. "I told him I'm not squeamish. I have six brothers, all of whom fought each other constantly just for the fun of it. I've helped staunch bleeding lips and noses for years." Lucinda took up a sandwich and bit into it with gusto. "Still, he says it's the house rules that women can't attend." She pursed her lips and frowned. "That is just silly."

"Alex told me the same thing." Emma picked up another sandwich but didn't bite into it. "Well, if the house rules say women can't attend, we won't attend." She gave Lucinda a sly look. "At least not as women."

Lucinda's eyes grew round and she leaned forward. "You have a way around the rules?"

"I believe I do, if you're willing to be a bit shocking." Emma wasn't certain if Alex's aunt would agree to the outrageous plan that had just popped into her head.

Lucinda sat up and laughed. "I'm an American, my dear. We were born to be shocking to the English."

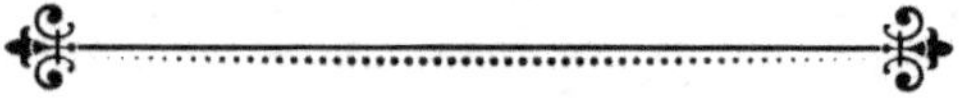

Chapter Fourteen

The day of the fight dawned bitterly cold. It hadn't warmed much by the time Alex arrived at Langham's at ten o'clock. The match was scheduled for eleven, and already carriages had begun to spill their occupants onto the sidewalk outside the Cambrian Stores. His relations were among the first people he recognized when he entered the upstairs arena. One entire section near the ropes was taken up by members of the Quartermain family. Trust that they would not be late for a wager.

"Well met, Alex." Grandfather was the first to greet him. "Can't tell you how exciting this match is going to be. I've got six different wagers going on at once." He grinned over at Tom. "And may have more before the fight is over."

"Good morning, Grandfather. I'm happy if I can brighten your day with a bet or two. Excuse me, please." Alex stalked over to Julius, book in hand. "You have all my wagers accounted for?"

"Morning, Alex." His cousin had a sour look on his face. "Do you doubt my ability to keep the wagers straight?"

"Not at all. But I'm staking a small fortune on this match. I just want to know everything has been taken care of." If he managed to win even half the wagers he'd placed on himself, he and Emma wouldn't need to worry about finances for a very long time to come.

"I assure you, everything you asked for has been entered."

Julius's face lightened. "Go knock 'em out, old chap."

"Will do, Jules." Alex nodded and headed for the dressing area, a roped off section in the far corner. He pulled back the curtain that gave the boxers a modicum of privacy to find his uncle already there, stripped to the waist, a slight smile on his face.

"Glorious morning, isn't it, nephew?" With his sleek physique and straight stance, Uncle Jack looked a much younger, more vigorous man than one would expect of his nearly fifty years. Make no mistake, this was going to be the fight of Alex's life in that ring.

"That it is, uncle." Quickly, Alex stripped out of his jacket and shirt, the chill of the air bringing goosebumps out all over his arms and chest. Concentrate on all the different combinations he'd practiced over the past two weeks. Langham himself had helped train Alex. His best advice had been to push all his emotion down into his stomach and let that power explode up through his arms.

His uncle peeped out from behind the curtain. "This ought to be a good show, Alex. They're packing them in like herrings in a basket."

That did little to calm Alex's nerves, but he refused to be intimidated either by the crowd or his uncle. "Then let the match begin."

Alex pushed his way past Uncle Jack, and the gentlemen in the audience roared their approval as he strode forward, winding his way through them to reach the ring. He climbed up through the ropes and headed to the corner behind which his family sat, wagers still being called out vigorously. His grandfather was standing, shouting at Tom, who laughed then turned to Jules and said, "Make it another hundred on that one."

Things would get even more hectic once the match began, but it always did when his family wagered.

Turning back to the ring, Alex bounced on his toes, trying to keep warm as Langham had taught him. Uncle Jack climbed up into the ring, and Langham himself came forward to act as referee. Two gentlemen who had sparred with both Jack and Alex during training had been designated their seconds and bottle-holders and they now took their positions on the floor directly behind the combatants.

Langham strode to the center of the ring and motioned both Jack and Alex to come toward him. "As always, may the best man win," he said, then stepped back.

Suddenly, Jack's face was in Alex's. Next thing he knew, pain exploded alongside his head and he tumbled backward onto the mat. So much for concentrating. Shaking it off, Alex crawled up on his knees, then to his feet, and surged forward, landing a blow on his uncle's chest.

Jack staggered back and Alex pressed forward, jabbing one, two, three times toward the face. His uncle managed to block the blows, so Alex changed tactics and led from the left, now aiming for the stomach. The first blow landed and he heard his uncle's "oof" distinctly.

Then Alex was looking up at Uncle Jack from the mat, his uncle reaching down to help him up with the assistance of his own second. There was a dull ringing in his ears as his second pulled him into his corner and knelt, giving Alex a seat on his knee as well as advice. "You're all right, Captain. Shake it off, just like Langham showed you. This is only the first round. You've got more to go. You'll land a good one on him, I know you will."

Slowly, the ringing in his ears subsided until he could clearly hear Sandy call to Julius for another wager. Well, if that was the case, Alex was likely all right.

Langham called, "Time!"

Alex stood, readying himself for another onslaught.

Movement to his right showed gentlemen still streaming into the already packed room. The latecomers, a large man with his boy looking almost frightened scurried to find places right behind the Quartermains. His family had been so loud and rowdy several gentlemen had moved to another part of the room. Nothing unusual there.

Steeling himself once more, Alex came forward to the middle of the ring. He had to find a way to get through his uncle's defenses or he'd be a good deal poorer by the time he left the ring. And exiled to Aldershot, teaching boxing for the rest of his time in the army. With that grim thought in mind, Alex stared into his uncle's eyes, heard Langham shout, "Time!" and came in swinging.

THE STEAMY SMELL of too many sweaty bodies assailed Emma the moment she and Lucinda entered the second-floor boxing chamber of the Cambrian Stores. She wrinkled her nose but continued onward into the room, determined to see her husband win this match.

At first, she'd been afraid they'd be found out and turned away. Their disguises—Lucinda as a portly gentleman and Emma as his young son—could only hide so much of their femininity, especially their faces. Lucinda had tried to don a false mustache, but it itched so much she scratched it off in the carriage on the way to the match. Nevertheless, the man at the door scarcely took a good look at them before waving them in, just two more gentlemen in the long line waiting to get in to witness the match.

Holding Lucinda's hand, Emma pushed her way through the crowd until she found a place to stand to get her bearings. Never had she suspected that so many gentlemen would wish to watch Alex and his uncle box. Did every gentleman in London enjoy boxing? Or were they drawn by the wagering that could be heard in every corner of the room—most loudly and virulently from the corner on her left. Those gentlemen seemed about to come to blows themselves regarding their non-stop call for bets, first on Alex, then on Jack.

"One would think gentlemen would be more polite about it."

Lucinda nodded to that same corner Emma had been staring at. "They seem overly enthusiastic about their wagering, so much so I don't think they're attending to the fight at all." She made a disgusted sound. "Not like gentlemen at all."

"Perhaps that's why they don't allow women to attend," Emma whispered, although no one likely could have heard her. "They don't have to act like gentlemen. They can be as rude and unappealing as they wish without ladies to make them at least attempt to be civilized. This bunch here is a good example. They're so rowdy no one wants to sit beside them."

As she spoke, several gentlemen standing behind the avid wagerers moved away from the annoying shouting to the other side of the room.

"Quick, Lucinda." Emma grabbed her hand again and tugged her toward the free space just relinquished.

"You want to stand next to those reprobates?" Lucinda dug her heels in. "Stop pulling. We're fine right here."

"We can see better from over there. Trust me. They may be loud, but at least they won't pay us any mind." That seemed to mollify her friend, and Lucinda followed her over to stand behind the gathering of noisy gentlemen.

Now Emma could concentrate on what was going on in the ring. It looked as if some of the boxing had been fierce. Alex was standing, but his shoulders were hunched, and his left eye looked swollen. Uncle Jack looked like he'd scarcely been touched and Emma had a sudden qualm, seeing herself in a rented flat in Aldershot for the rest of her life. But no, she had to have faith in her husband. They'd made the sacrifice of two eternal weeks without a bit of physical comfort between them. So yes, Alex was going to beat the stuffing out of his uncle. That was all there was to it.

"Speed it up, Alex," one of the gentlemen in front of them called out. "You know I've got a packet riding on you."

"No more than I do, Tom," another one called out.

"If you knock him out this round, Alex, I'll be set for life."

"Don't listen to Francis, Alex. He's wagering Jack will get you in this round."

Emma hoped Alex couldn't hear their rude comments. Serve that Francis right if he did lose. Wait. Francis? And Tom. Heart in her throat, Emma peered closer at the gentlemen in front of her. Oh, dear God. She tugged on Lucinda's hand. "It's the Quartermains."

"Who are the Quartermains?" She looked confused.

"The men in front of us."

"But who are they?"

"Alex's cousins."

Lucinda reared back and stared at Emma as if she wanted to shake her. "I *told* you not to come over here." A glance around the room and she came back to Emma, lips pursed. "There's nowhere else to go. If they see you, they're bound to recognize you. We'll be ruined."

"I don't think we'll be ruined. We're married women, there's nothing we haven't seen really. But I don't think they'll see us, Lucinda. They're more interested in their wagering and the fight to consider turning around and looking at us."

After gazing at the Quartermains, who were busying themselves with their betting calls, plainly not paying attention to anything else, Lucinda nodded. "I suspect you're right. They won't know we're even here unless we call attention to ourselves." She glanced up at the ring and gripped Emma's arm. "Look, they're starting again."

"Time!" A gentleman Emma didn't know yelled out, then quickly left the ring.

Alex darted forward, landing a solid blow to Uncle Jack's jaw. The older man staggered backward but didn't go down. Instead, he raced back toward Alex and brought his arm upward with power Emma could see plainly from where she stood. The blow caught Alex under the chin, lifted him off his feet and against the ropes.

Without thought, Emma shrieked, the sound high and thin.

Unmistakably female. She clamped her hands over her mouth, but the sound couldn't be recalled.

Every head in the Quartermain clan turned to look at her in the quiet that ensued.

Hoping her words about not being ruined would still be true, she burrowed her face into Lucinda's ample bosom and prayed.

THE UNMISTAKABLE SOUND of his wife's shriek brought Alex to his senses like a bucket of cold water poured over his head. Damn, but the woman wouldn't listen to him at all. Anger toward her and his opponent bubbled up from deep within Alex. He needed to end this now so he could deal with his wife. Preferably over his knee with her bare backside showing.

That image sent a surge of unbridled desire through his body, more powerful than the anger that ran alongside it. Langham's training came to the forefront of his mind, and instinctively, he hit Jack with a two-point combination: a straight punch to the gut followed by a powerhouse right hook to the head. His uncle shrugged off the gut-punch, but the hook caught him in exactly the right place on the jaw. Uncle Jack went down as though he'd been poleaxed.

Alex continued to bounce on the balls of his feet, waiting for his uncle to rise. He didn't. His second scurried forward to try and bring him around.

Langham came over and began the count.

Then a scream shook the room. A large gentleman hurried down toward the ring, followed closely by a young boy. Except it wasn't a young boy at all. It was Emma.

"Time." Langham turned to Alex. "I declare Captain Bancroft the winner of this match."

A shout went up all over the room, the buzz of noise being loudest in the corner behind Alex. Dazed by everything that had just happened, he peered over at his uncle, who seemed to be coming to, assisted by his second and the large gentleman he'd seen earlier. An air of strangeness made his head spin until Emma appeared and threw herself into his arms.

"I'm so sorry, my love. With so much at stake, I couldn't stay away."

Immediately, Alex pulled her away, his head clearing. He had to get her out of here before she was discovered. "You must leave now, Emma. We will speak of this, *at length*, tonight, but you must get away before you are found out." He nodded to the man assisting his uncle to stand. "Who is that man who came with you?"

She gazed up at him, fear suddenly in her eyes. "Lucinda."

Dear God. If anything happened to his pregnant wife, Uncle Jack would mop the floor with Alex for sure. "Go to her and make her leave. Tell her I will bring Uncle Jack home, but you both must leave, *now*.

Emma hesitated, glancing from him to his aunt.

"Go!"

She started toward Aunt Lucinda, and after some struggle, managed to pull her away from his uncle. They left the ring, and he thanked God when they finally disappeared out the door.

Meanwhile, the room had erupted into cheers and whistles. His cousins were still haggling over their bets, but he saw slips of IOUs being passed back and forth, so everything seemed to have worked itself out. After he changed, he'd seek out Jules and collect his winnings.

He'd won. Alex had scarcely taken that in yet. He wasn't going to have to spend his life teaching this dreadful sport to other unwitting soldiers. Emma's dowry was intact, and they now had an estate. Grinning from ear to ear, Alex headed over to his uncle's corner, where the man was drinking water and blinking rapidly.

"So the best man won, nephew." His uncle looked up at him and winced as he moved his jaw. "That's a devilish right hook you've got there. I'm proud of you, even though I'll be eating blancmange for a week."

"I hope not, uncle. You'll be fine in a day or two, unless Aunt Lucinda takes you to task for getting injured." Alex wondered if she'd already done so just now. "Can you stand?"

Slowly, his uncle rose, and Alex took his arm. "You may be getting too old for this sort of thing."

"Nonsense, my boy." He winced as he started to move, Alex's arm around his shoulders. "I've never felt better."

"I suppose you must feel miserable all the time then." Alex laughed and Uncle Jack joined in. They climbed down from the ring, making their way toward the dressing area through throngs of congratulatory spectators.

"Tell me something, Alex." His uncle limped as he went behind the curtain. "Who was that gentleman who tried to assist me when I couldn't get up? I didn't recognize him, but then I was so dizzy at that point I couldn't see straight. Do I know him?"

Laughing, Alex thumped Uncle Jack on the back. "Yes, uncle, you know him. Allow me to let you in on a little secret."

AFTER SETTLING HIS wagers with Julius, Alex arrived home in a happier mood than he'd had in many weeks. He'd won the estate free and clear from Uncle Jack, Emma's fortune was intact, and his own had grown substantially in the past several hours. Once his commission was refunded from the army, they would be on solid financial footing to begin their new life in Shropshire.

The only thing marring his joy was the knowledge that Emma had disobeyed him in a spectacular fashion. By attending the boxing match not only had she gone against his wishes, but she'd exposed herself to rowdy men with coarse language unfit for a lady's ears. Not to mention the dangers Lucinda had been subject to in her delicate condition. Had they been recognized—and he wouldn't know that for days until the gossip about the match circulated through the *ton*—both families might have to slink off to the country and wait for Society to forget this transgression.

Now, despite his exhilarated spirits, he would have to play the stern husband and devise a punishment for his disobedient wife.

The butler opened the door for him with, "Congratulations on your victory, Captain Bancroft."

"Thank you, Buckleigh." Well, news did travel fast these days. "Is my wife at home?" She'd better be.

"Yes, sir. I believe she has repaired to the bedchamber."

"Very good." Best deal with this now. No need to put it off. "There may be some callers this afternoon, gentlemen wanting to render their congratulations as well. I am not home to anyone for the rest of the day, Buckleigh. Is that understood?"

"Perfectly, sir." The butler bowed and Alex headed up the stairs to confront his recalcitrant wife.

The door to their chamber was ajar. Alex paused to put his sternest face on, then pushed it open.

Emma sat on the chaise longue in her nightgown, all trace of the boyish masquerade gone. As he entered, she looked up, bit her lip, and rose. "May I offer my congratulations on your victory?"

Alex strode toward her, his mouth opened to scold her soundly. But her soft voice, the sweet smell of jasmine that swirled around her, and the look of adoration in her eyes banished his rebuke. Instead, he grabbed her head in his hands and his mouth descended onto hers. God, he had missed kissing her. And touching her. He ran his hands over her luscious form, reveling in the feel of her.

No, no, he needed to admonish her for her blatant disobedience. Alex broke the kiss and stared down at his flushed and aroused wife. It had been a long two weeks, but she had to understand—

"I know it was wrong of me to go to the match, Alex." Emma gazed up at him, true repentance on her face. "But with so much at stake for our lives, I wanted to be there. Needed to be near you." Her bottom lip began to quiver. "Can you forgive me?"

How could he ever remain angry at that beautiful face? "You have no idea how I felt when I heard you shriek, Emma. I knew immediately it could only be you."

"You did?" Her face lit up as though he'd given her a gift.

"Of course I did. And the first thing I thought to do was put you over my knee and paddle your bare bottom for disobeying me." That image of her naked backside aroused him yet again. It had been a very long two weeks without her in his bed.

Despite his vivid words, she smiled and took his hand. "I can think of better ways to use this than spanking the mother of your child."

Eyes widening, his gaze dropping to her stomach, Alex opened his mouth but no sound emerged. After some gasping breaths, he finally managed, "You're really carrying my child?"

She nodded happily. "I am, my love. Another reason why I am so very thankful you are not going to India. I want you here when your son is born."

"But how can you be certain? Have you seen a doctor?" She'd not been sick in the mornings; he knew that well enough sharing a bed with her for four months.

"No, but I am certain." She cocked her head and smiled at him. "In all the time since our wedding night, have you ever known me to have my courses?"

Surprised, Alex blinked and thought back. "No, never."

"Up until our wedding day, they came with a regimented predictability." She beamed at him. "But not for the last four months. So I'd say, Captain Bancroft, that along about the end of May or the first of June, someone will be calling you Papa."

Alex's heart swelled at the thought of a child coming, of becoming a true family. And he'd be here to see it happen and watch him or her grow up. "Oh, darling." He grabbed her to him and squeezed gently. "You have truly made me the happiest of men."

Emma pulled his head down until she could whisper in his ear, "If you want me to be the happiest of women, take me to bed, Alex. It's been much too long."

Laughing loudly, Alex scooped her up into his arms and carried her over to the big bed he'd missed so much. "Your wish is my command, my love."

EPILOGUE

Shropshire
July, 1861

WARM SUNSHINE STREAMING through the trees dappled the lawn stretching out behind Red Fox Manor. Alex had ordered a table and chairs set up on the back terrace for him and Emma and their guests, Uncle Jack and Aunt Lucinda, to enjoy the fresh air each day of their visit. They'd spent the past week catching up on all the news since he and Emma had moved to Shropshire after Christmas.

"How is your boxing coming, uncle? Any more wager matches?" Alex couldn't help teasing his uncle. If Alex never boxed again in his life, he'd be a supremely happy man.

"I actually did have an exhibition match with Langham." Jack grinned at him. "Suggested by your cousin Lord Boxted. The family apparently enjoyed our match so much, they wanted another chance to wager on a fight." His uncle fixed him with a glint in his eye. "You wouldn't be interested in a re-match, would you? Your cousin says there would be thousands of pounds to be made from such a match. I'm ready if you are."

"Certainly not, uncle." Emma spoke up before Alex could open his mouth. "With a new family to tend to and an estate to run, Alex's days as a boxer are ended for good."

"I wish I could say the same for Jack." Lucinda stirred her tea and glanced at her husband fondly. "After the twins were born, I'd hoped he'd quit the ring in favor of spending more time in the nursery." She sipped, then added more sugar. "Unfortunately, that has not happened."

"Having two babies at once must be a special blessing." Emma sounded wistful. "Our John is the light of my life, but I so want him to have a little brother or sister."

Uncle Jack's face lit up as he turned to Alex. "Well, nephew? I've never heard of a better wager."

"What?" Lost in gazing at his wife, more beautiful to him now that she was the mother of his child, Alex hadn't been paying close attention. "What do you want to wager on, uncle?"

"Who will be the first of us to have another child, of course." His uncle sat back, arms crossed over his chest, grinning like a fool.

"Jack!" Blushing, Lucinda slapped his shoulder.

The wager took Alex aback. Rather indelicate, but that had never stopped his uncle before. Sheepishly, he turned to Emma to find her face red, but a smile on her lips. A scant nod, and her cheeks grew even redder.

A satisfied smirk on his face, Alex leaned back in his chair and crossed his arms in imitation of his uncle. This was a wager he'd be more than happy to take up. And unlike their last one, this one he'd be willing to repeat for as long as his uncle cared to wager. "Very well, uncle."

He blew a kiss to Emma, who blushed again. They would begin working on winning this wager tonight. "You're on."

The End

About the Author

Jenna Jaxon is a best-selling author of historical romance, writing in a variety of time periods because she believes that passion is timeless. She has been reading and writing historical romance since she was a teenager. A romantic herself, Jenna has always loved a dark side to the genre, a twist, suspense, a surprise. She tries to incorporate all these elements into her own stories.

She lives in Virginia with her family and a small menagerie of pets—including two vocal cats, one almost silent cat, two curious bunnies, and a Shar-pei mix named Frenchie.

Blog: www.jennajaxon.wordpress.com
Facebook: facebook.com/jenna.jaxon
Twitter: @Jenna_Jaxon
Instagram: passionistimeless
TikTok: @jennajaxon1

www.ingramcontent.com/pod-product-compliance
Lightning Source LLC
Chambersburg PA
CBHW070400200726
48294CB00003B/1006

* 9 7 8 1 9 6 0 1 8 4 9 3 1 *